THE AWAKENING

New Journeys

ISBN: 1517494842
ISBN 13: 9781517494841

Again, I must say THANK YOU to Linda Keltz who reads my scribbles and gets it all typed into the computer. I haven't told her yet that I am working on another book. I have a fear of seeing her run down the street screaming – no, no, no!

I also must thank my dear wife Carol Ann. She handles all of the exchanges with the publisher and makes suggestions here and there. I couldn't do it without both of you ladies.

Elliott

DEDICATION

This book is the final volume of the JOURNEYS TRILOGY.

It is dedicated to our Grandson Cody Lee Brake. Cody was born with what will be a life long handicap which he strives to overcome every day.

Many thanks are due for his parents Terrill and Bette Kay as well as Cody's brothers, Jason and Kalen for their unfailing support.

Love
Granpa

Chapter 1 2156

It was June and on a warm afternoon Chris was sitting under an umbrella on the deck with a glass of iced tea in front of him. Carol was resting in the house and Chris planned to use the quiet time to start reading the accounts of Phoebe, Brendon and Melinda's first days after the great disaster in 2106. He had taken the discs they had given him and had them transcribed and printed. There were three thick folders on the table and since he had met Mel before the other two he decided to read her story first. The accounts had been written in a narrative style rather than as a first person accounting of the events.

Chapter 2 2106

It was mid-morning. Melinda was taking a shower in her new apartment at the University of Chicago Medical Center. She had left the bathroom door open. Gradually the entire apartment took on a red glow which quickly turned to blinding white flash. It was as if a dozen photo lamps had been set off at the same time. Putting on a robe Melinda inspected her apartment. Everything appeared normal with no sign of a flash fire. There had been no noise so it could not have been an explosion. Looking out of the window from her third floor level she could see nothing amiss. As she continued to look she saw two cars in the next block which appeared to have had a head-on collision. Looking in the opposite direction she spotted another car which had driven off the street and rammed into the front of a building. As she watched, Campus Police cars responded to both accidents. Seeing that the situation was under control, Melinda returned to preparing herself for the day. She dressed, ate cold cereal for breakfast then watched videos until it was time to go to work at 3:00pm.

At 2:30 Melinda left her apartment for the 3 block walk to work. She was currently working in the emergency room and in a month was scheduled to begin her residency in Geriatric medicine. When the elevator refused to answer the call button for the third floor Melinda walked down the stairs. On entering the lobby Melinda saw one of her neighbors lying in the open elevator door. She hurried over and after checking his vital signs she determined that the man was dead. Looking around the lobby Melinda could see into the Manager's office where the manager sat slumped at her desk with her head and shoulders down on the desk. Again there was no sign of life. Melinda picked up the phone and dialed the campus emergency number. There was no response and after several attempts she took out her cell phone which also got no response. Beginning to feel a sense of panic she walked out to the street only to have her fears increased. As she looked up and down the street there were several bodies within a half block of her location. She checked two bodies which were close to where she came out to the street. Both of them were dead and in fact both of them were already cool to the touch. Melinda became aware of how utterly silent it was. The silence was broken only by the occasional cry by one of the ever present gulls soaring overhead.

Melinda set off at a brisk walk for the Emergency Room, passing more bodies along the way. At the hospital she could not believe what she was seeing. The waiting room, nurses' station and hallway were all littered with bodies. It appeared as if they had all died with no warning. There was no sign of trauma or panic. They had been alive one moment and dead the next. Melinda checked out part of the hospital and found the same scenario everywhere she looked.

Melinda stood at the Emergency Room entrance and contemplated her next move. She finally decided to return to her apartment where she could relax and consider her options. On arriving home she soon discovered there was no radio, television or phone service. The cell phone indicated no services so she felt truly isolated.

Suddenly frightened, Melinda locked the dead bolt on her door. She then took her rifle out of the bedroom closet and loaded it. It was the first time the rifle had been out of the case since she arrived in Chicago. It was a light weight .223 caliber, late model lever action weapon with which she was quite proficient. It was capable, with a well-placed shot, of stopping a deer sized animal including, she thought with a shudder, a man.

Melinda wasn't hungry but knew she needed to eat. She opened a can of soup and put a can of freezer biscuits in the oven. As she was eating the realization came to her that she was going to have to leave and sooner rather than later. In a few days the odor from decaying bodies would become over-powering in the closed up apartment building.

Melinda slept surprisingly well that night. She wakened early next morning and set about preparing to leave. There was a small day pack in the closet, but Melinda quickly saw it would not be sufficient for her needs. Recalling a sporting goods store nearby she set out on a shopping trip. The store was only a few blocks away from the apartment and had catered to students of the university. As she started for the door Melinda stopped, returned and picked up her riffle.

The heft of the weapon in her hand was a familiar sensation which put Melinda at ease. It took her back to the days of her youth in Montana and the Dakotas. She set out with a confident swing to her step and was soon at the store. Entering the unlocked door she took out the list she had written and began shopping. Beginning with a backpack and an ultra-light sleeping bag she soon completed her list. She adjusted the straps on the pack and placed the other items inside. She would do the final packing that night at home.

Almost as soon as she started down the street for home Melinda had a feeling she was being followed. She immediately checked her rifle to be sure it was loaded then continued on her way. Twice she started and shied away from her own image reflected in store windows. After the second time she sat down on a bench at a bus top to calm herself and settle her nerves. As her breathing and heart rate returned to normal she became aware of a clicking noise. Looking around for the source of the noise she soon spotted a small dog approaching. The animal had a wiry coat, brown head and ears and a stub of a tail. It also had a couple of brown spots on the body. Melinda was not an expert on dog breeds but she recognized this one as a Jack Russell Terrier. The dog walked out into the street and sat down about fifteen feet from Melinda. It sat with ears up and eyes never leaving the woman's face. After perhaps half a minute Melinda snapped her fingers and said, "Come," at which point the dog trotted over and sat down at her feet. After a few seconds Melinda patted her lap and the dog instantly leaped up, all wiggles and trying to cover Melinda's face with kisses. Melinda had noticed that the dog was female and was wearing two collars. One appeared to be a plastic flea collar while the other was leather with three small metal tags attached. One of the tags was a current rabies tag, one was a 2106 license which the third held the name Maggie and an address from about a mile away.

Melinda put the dog back on the sidewalk and stood up. She said, "It looks as if we have adopted each other Maggie so let's go home and pack. We have a lot of miles to cover." Passing a pet supply store in the next block Melinda went in. She found a retractable leash, a ten pound bag of dry dog food and a small plastic food dish. She also searched for and found a pet nail clipper which went into the pack with the other items.

When they arrived at the apartment Melinda fed the dog which appeared to be extremely hungry. She then began sorting through her possessions to determine which she could take and what she must leave behind. It soon became apparent that clothing and food would take up most of the room in her pack. She had an extensive collection of arrowheads and stone axes which, sadly, would have to be left behind. There was a bear claw necklace and a red stone calumet which had belonged to her family for 250 years. These two items were wrapped in bath towels and carefully placed in the bottom of the pack. In an effort to keep her pack as light as possible Melinda packed a minimum of clothing. She was sure she could find anything she might need along the way. She planned to walk in her hiking boots, shorts and a light weight shirt. Late in the afternoon Maggie began dancing at the door. Malinda snapped on the leash and they went outside. There was a grass strip between the sidewalk and the street. Maggie was allowed to do her business there. Melinda made no effort to clean up the waste. It made no sense to pick up the droppings and put them in a can which would probably never be emptied.

They returned to the apartment where Melinda was sure she could already smell the bodies in and around the building. She fed Maggie again and prepared a salad and a sandwich for herself. After eating, the road atlas was brought out and Melinda began to plot her way home. She decided to follow US 90 until in intersected with US 20 and then stay on US 20 all of the way to Sioux City. From there she would take US 29 north to Waterton where she would change to US 212 going west. US 212 ran through the heart of the Cheyenne River Reservation. If any of her people had survived she felt this was where she would find them. She checked the contents of her pack again then stood it near the door. All she would need to add in the morning would be bathroom articles and water for the two canteens which she would tie to the pack rather than her belt. At about 8 pm she took Maggie out for the last time then indulged in a long hot shower which might be the last for several days. Using an old blanket she made a bed for Maggie. After some coaxing the dog seem to grasp that it was for her. After the dog was settled Melinda went to her own bed and turned out the light. In less than a minute Maggie jumped onto the bed, circled a couple of times and with a sigh snuggled up to Melinda's hip and promptly began to make a soft snoring sound. The presence of the dog was somehow comforting and Melinda allowed her to stay.

Next morning Melinda awoke to the sound of rain pelting against the windows. She quickly decided this would not be a good day to start her long hike. Maggie was dancing to go out so Melinda put on her rain jacket, snapped on the leash and they went downstairs. The leash was long enough to span the sidewalk so Melinda stayed in the shelter of the doorway and let Maggie go out alone. The day passed slowly. Melinda paced about the apartment until the dog, which apparently sensed her feeling of unease, began to pace with her. In mid-afternoon the rain finally stopped and the sun came out. Melinda snapped the leash on Maggie and they set out for a walk. There was a faint unpleasant, odor in the air which Melinda soon identified as coming from the decaying bodies which littered the sidewalks. They saw no one living and after covering 8 or 10 blocks returned to the apartment. Melinda found it difficult to believe that everyone in Chicago had perished, but that certainly seemed to be the case in her neighborhood. She wondered whether the event, whatever it was, had extended across the country. The only means of finding the answer was to go and see. She had briefly considered trying to find a vehicle to drive but the question of finding fuel or charging stations had dissuaded her from that idea. In addition, she was not a very experienced driver. As a youth she had walked everywhere she wanted to go and was confident she could walk the eight hundred or so miles to get home. Melinda retired early with Maggie once again snuggled up to her hip. Her last thought before sleep took her was to wonder if her husband Brad had survived in Seattle.

Chapter 3 2106

On April 10, the fourth morning after the great die-off as Melinda thought of the event, she wakened as the sun rose. She prepared a larger than usual breakfast with the thought that she would not need to stop for lunch. At 7:00 am Melinda set off with Maggie on the leash. There was bright sunshine and it held the promise of a warm spring day. In addition to her pack, Melinda had put on a heavy belt which held a small hand axe, a hunting knife with a six inch blade and a Ruger .22 caliber semi-automatic pistol. She had owned the pistol since she was a young teen ager but had not fired it since coming to Chicago to start college. It was a short mile and a half from the apartment to the highway and they were soon headed north on US 90. There were numerous cars on the roadway. Some had been stopped and many more were entangled in multiple vehicle crashes. The smell of decaying bodies was quite pronounced where there were several cars involved. The odor appeared to upset Maggie and she cowered close to Melinda's leg while they were passing those scenes. Melinda had tried to maintain a brisk pace all day but had been forced to slow down as she worked her way through the many piles of wrecked autos At 5:00 pm she was approaching an intersection where US 94 split off and turned north. She estimated they had covered some 15 or 16 miles. Her legs and shoulders were crying for relief and she was sure Maggie was tired as well. There were numerous motels along the surface streets bordering the freeway so she exited and began searching for a room. She bypassed the first two motels because there were bodies lying about the parking lots and a tangle of cars in front of the offices. On her third try she found a small two story affair which advertised "30 Clean Rooms" on its street sign. She looked in and saw two bodies in the office. Looking around she saw a house cleaner's cart beside an open door on the ground floor. Melinda went to investigate. She found the room empty and while the bed was unmade there were clean sheets piled on it. The bathroom had apparently been cleaned and there were clean towels hanging on the rods. The housekeeper's key was still in the lock so Melinda put it in her pocket and decided the room would do nicely. The electricity was still on and there was hot water. Melinda thought those were things which would soon change. Melinda locked Maggie in the room and went in search of food. In the manager's apartment she found a well-stocked freezer and pantry. She took a roast beef frozen dinner, a box of fried chicken and two cans of mixed fruit then returned to her room. She heated the dinner and while she was eating did the same with the chicken which would go into a plastic bag for tomorrow. After eating she took Maggie out for a short walk. She then filled the tub with water as hot as she could tolerate. She submerged her aching body in the tub and stayed until the water began to cool.

Sleep came instantly when Melinda turned off the light. She was awakened just after dawn by a brilliant flash of lightning which was followed by a rolling clap of thunder. The thunder seemed to shake the building. The curtains had been left open and Melinda could see and hear the rain pounding against the windows. She stayed in bed drifting in and out of sleep. Eventually the storm drifted away but a steady drizzle of rain continued. Maggie began dancing and yipping at the door with the need to go out. Melinda decided to let the dog out without the leash, confident that she would not go far. Standing in the door she watched the dog nose around, take care of her business and hurry back to the shelter of the room. Apparently, Maggie didn't relish being wet and cold any more than did Melinda.

It was obvious they were not going to be traveling that day so Melinda returned to the manager's apartment in search of breakfast. In the kitchen she found eggs, sausage, bread and a jar of jam. She cooked these and even scrambled of couple of eggs to give Maggie a change from the dry food diet.

Looking around the apartment Melinda saw a well-stocked bookcase. After browsing through the titles she selected three volumes. All of these were small books as she had to consider the weight she was adding to her pack. The three books were historical treatises which dealt with events on the Great Plains in the late 19th century. The day passed uneventfully and the next morning held promise of a bright and sunny day.

They were on the road early and Melinda set a goal of twenty miles for the day. There were fewer wrecked or abandoned cars on this stretch of highway and they made good time. Melinda was alert for any sign of human life but saw none. They rested for a half hour at noon and were on their way again. At 5:00 pm they were approaching the intersection with US 290.

Chapter 4 2106

Melinda decided they had walked enough for the day so they exited the highway and entered a rest area adjacent to the two interstates. There were only five vehicles in the parking lot. There were a number of bodies lying outside the visitor center and several more inside and in the ladies' restroom. She tried the men's room and found it empty so she made use of it and returned outside. She found a camper van in the parking lot which was not locked and which held no bodies. They spent a restful night and were on the road early the next morning. Melinda changed her travel strategy. She was no longer going to set a mileage goal for each day. She was simply going to walk until she was tired then start looking for a suitable place to spend the night. They never had to spend a night outside and on June 2 they were approaching the little Iowa town of Dike. Any time they were within a half mile of a population center the stench of decomposing bodies was overpowering. It seemed to affect Maggie more than Melinda. Melinda learned that when Maggie began looking around and crowding against her legs they were approaching a scene of dead bodies. Dike was located a quarter mile from the highway and as they entered the town Maggie seemed more relaxed than usual. They found a small house on the edge of town which held no bodies. They settled into the house and had their evening meal. After eating, Melinda decided to take a look at the little town. She put the leash on Maggie and took her rifle with her. As they walked the street toward the center of town she became aware of bones lying on the overgrown lawns. She thought it odd that the bodies had been reduced to bare bones in less than a month. As she turned a corner onto the main business street she immediately saw the reason for the bones. The street was alive with thirty or forty vultures and probably twenty coyotes squabbling over the remains of a half dozen corpses. The scavengers took little notice of the human intruder who instantly stopped and then reversed her steps. Melinda returned to the house. After entering she checked to make sure every door and window was closed and locked. Melinda spent a restless night.

In the morning she fed Maggie, put on the leash and drank a cup of coffee while the dog explored the front yard to the extent the leash allowed her. They were on the road at an early hour and made good time. In early afternoon they entered the town of Wellsberg and Melinda decided they had traveled far enough for the day. The business district was on the highway and was only three blocks long. The bodies visible on the street had been reduced to bones. It was evident that the scavengers had been at work. She proceeded through the town without stopping until a short distance west of the city limit sign. Here she spotted a small, neat looking house which was set back from the road a hundred yards or so. As she walked up the driveway there were numerous bones scattered about. The house was unlocked and there were no bodies inside. Melinda took off her pack and leaned it against the wall. She considered how fortunate she had been in finding shelter every night. That would surely change when she started out across the South Dakota prairie. The yard was fenced so she let Maggie go outside without the leash. There was a well-stocked freezer and pantry. The property was equipped with a solar array so there was power and hot water. There was a small fenced garden. After six weeks it was overgrown with weeds but it held a variety of vegetables. Melinda was starved for fresh produce and she made use of the garden bounty. She stayed for four days then reluctantly took to the road.

The days seemed to melt together. There were no major events, the landscape was flat or gently rolling and it seemed as if she had been walking forever. The presence of Maggie alleviated some of the boredom. The dog often darted after the occasional ground squirrel or rabbit which bounced out of the roadside grass. They slept under a roof every night and twice, when they found a place which was really comfortable, they stayed over for a day. On the 20th of June as they approached the little town of Sac City, Melinda spotted the buildings of a small farm just east of the town across a narrow river. She turned in the yard when she saw outside lights burning. She could see a solar array on a gentle hill behind the buildings. There were bones lying about the yard but upon entering the unlocked house she discovered no bodies. There was water pressure and hot water which caused Melinda to decide to stay for a couple of days. There was a layer of dust on everything so Melinda found the cleaning supplies and in an hour the kitchen and bedroom were clean with fresh linen on the bed. Melinda made her supper that evening from eggs she found in the refrigerator. She was suspicious of them but when she cracked a couple they looked and smelled as she thought they should. There was bread and butter from the freezer a jar of jam from the pantry. She even scrambled a couple of eggs for Maggie. She took a long hot shower and while drying her hair decided she was going to cut it short. She had never carried much excess fat and two months of walking had left her trim and fit. The bathroom scales indicated a weight of 116 pounds, about what she had weighed at age 16. She retired early that night and slept very well. She was awakened early by Maggie's routine of dancing and yipping to go out. After another shower and breakfast Melinda examined the house thoroughly. There was another small bedroom and in what had most likely been the master bedroom was an office. There were two desks and one wall covered by a bookcase which was filled with law books. Further examination revealed the names of Jessica and Frank Williams both of whom had been attorneys. The room also held a full spectrum of video and sound equipment plus a large collection of videos and music recordings. Melinda spent a good part of the day dusting and cleaning the house. She spent a half hour throwing a tennis ball in the back yard for Maggie to fetch. Over the next two days Melinda examined the other buildings on the property. One of them was a well house which held a pump, plus valves controlling water to the house and other structures. There was detailed instructions for draining the irrigation system for the yard and garden plus setting the timing and amount of water for irrigating. The garden was overgrown with weeds but there was still a bounty of vegetables available for the picking.

In a larger building with two double doors she found a charging grid with a number of vehicles connected to it. There was a small truck, a large ATV, a lawn mower, a garden tractor and even a snow mobile. All of the vehicles indicated that they were fully charged. There was no livestock on the place and no indication that it had ever held any.

After a week Melinda asked herself why she was still there. The answer was that she was comfortable and that she was tired of traveling. Besides, she told herself, there was little chance she would find anyone if she walked to her old home in South Dakota. She decided on the spot she was going to stay. As it turned out, she stayed for three years.

It was only late June but Melinda thought she had better prepare herself for the long winter which would be upon her in a few months. She cautiously backed the little truck out of the garage and after testing the brakes set out for Sac City which was just across the bridge. Driving through the town twice to acquaint herself with the layout of a place she took note of the locations of two grocery stores and a pharmacy. On the front of the small brick building was a sign with the word, Williams-Attorneys. Apparently her deceased hosts had an office besides the one at home. Melinda entered one of the grocery stores and was struck with the neatness of the place. She encountered only two bodies and both of them had passed the stage of terrible stench and had begun to mummify. The electricity was out in the building so all of the meat and dairy products had long since spoiled. It occurred to Melinda that when winter came all of the canned goods would freeze and be lost as well. She went to the second grocery store and found the same situation as at the first. At the pharmacy she immediately began to fill a cart with medical supplies of every sort. Melinda spent the next three weeks hauling groceries and household supplies with the little truck. She stored all of it in the garage which was heated or cooled as the weather dictated when she was finished the garage resembled a warehouse.

Next Melinda attacked the yard. The grass was well over a foot tall and was going to seed. She raised the mower to the highest setting for the first cutting then lowered it for a second cut. She attached a tiller to the garden tractor and went over the garden. Water to the garden was turned off to discourage any more weed growth.

Melinda discovered that Jessica had been about her own size and there was a substantial amount of good clothing for both summer and winter. The shoes and boots were too large but a trip into Sac City resolved that problem. She was even able to find hiking boots of the same make and style as those in which she had walked from Chicago.

The rest of the summer passed quickly as one day followed another. Except for meat Melinda had several years supply of food stored in the garage. Meat was readily available on the hoof so she had no concern on that account. In addition to cattle and swine there were many deer and turkeys in the area. She saw both almost every day from the deck on the north side of the house. She spent considerable time on the deck reading and listening to music. She also enjoyed just sitting and looking at the view of the river valley to the north. The only real problems she faced were sheer loneliness and feral dogs. There was no cure for the loneliness except to keep her mind occupied and that was not always easy to accomplish. The other problem was feral dogs. She saw only medium to large sized dogs which seemed to run in packs of five or six animals. The dogs were very aggressive and attacked without any provocation. She never ventured into town without her rifle and never went out of the house without the Ruger pistol. Melinda had shot and killed a number of the dogs and came to look at them as being no different than any wild predator.

The first killing frost occurred in the middle of September. Melinda thought this was at least five or six weeks earlier than normal but she heeded the warning. She turned off all of the outside water lines and drained the systems. On one of her walks, which she took almost daily, she had seen a small orchard west of Sac City. There were only ten trees which still held apples. She took the little truck, a ladder and a basket and soon had five or six bushels of rather wormy apples. She peeled, cored and cut out the worm damage then cooked them down for applesauce. She canned the rest.

Melinda had scoured the town for gardens and she spent the last half of September harvesting potatoes, carrots, onions and one small plot of parsnips. There were even a small number of tomatoes which the frost had not ruined. She was out of freezer space and still had no meat put away. She went shopping for a freezer. The problem was getting the unit moved after she found one. At a furniture store she found an electric powered truck with a tailgate lift. After much struggle she managed to get two upright freezers moved into her garage. She had seen hogs eating the discards from the apples she had processed. She had dumped the discards behind one of the out buildings and the hogs continued to return to the spot even after the apple refuse was gone. She shot two medium sized animals from the herd. Butchering the animals was no different than dressing a deer which she had done many times in South Dakota. The beef was the same operation on a larger scale. She had obtained several knives and two saws from the local meat market. By the end of the first week in October she was finished and she felt she was as prepared for winter as she could be.

A week after she had finished with the meat processing she awoke one morning to discover the temperature had dropped twenty degrees and there were four inches of snow on the ground. The snow continued unabated for two days and the wind blew most of that time. Going anywhere was out of the question. At times visibility was zero. She could not see the garage which sat only 75 feet from the house. When the snow ended the temperature stood at zero. Melinda could see the river had already begun to freeze over along the edges. The rest of the year passed with the weather pattern of late October continuing. Bitter cold lay over the land with one snowstorm following the previous one. Melinda became frightened and began to wonder if the snow and cold would ever relent.

Chapter 5 2107-2108

With the New Year the weather changed dramatically. The temperature reached the high thirties almost every day. Much of the snow melted and Melinda began a walking routine. She covered five miles every day and occasionally stretched that to twelve or fifteen. Twice she spent the night in roadside houses or stores. Without heat or lights these were not very comfortable events so she made a point of heading for home with adequate time to get there before dark.

In February the severe weather returned and Melinda's daily walks had to be discontinued. She continued to exercise by putting in two hours each day riding a stationary bicycle she found in a storage building and wrestled into the house. While she was on the bike she passed the time listening to audio books from the sizable library in the home.

March brought a marked change in the weather. By the middle of the month the frost was gone from the ground and the leaf buds were swelling on the trees. The most cheering event was the appearance of the first Robins and Bluebirds. When Melinda heard the first Robin call as it searched for worms in the yard she danced a little jig and laughed out loud.

Melinda was starved for fresh greens and other vegetables. She ran the tiller over the garden to loosen the soil then planted a variety of seeds on April first. She wondered about the eight foot fence around the garden until she saw deer hopping over six foot fences along the highway.

Spring and summer passed with no noteworthy events. Melinda often thought about home in South Dakota but gave no serious thought to starting out again.

Melinda was becoming restless. She finally made the decision to make the rest of the trek to South Dakota in 2109.

She again planted the produce plus putting pork and beef in the freezer. She fretted through the fall and early winter with the desire to be on the road again.

Chapter 6 2109

The winter was another severe one with much snow and bitter cold. Melinda and Maggie were comfortable in the little house but Melinda began to detest the sight of the bike yet she spent two hours and at times three or four pedaling while listening to audio books. She gave much thought to what she would do if she reached home and found no one there. She finally decided she would simply return to this place, prepared to live out her life alone. She was confident she could make the one way trip in a little more than a month if she averaged fifteen miles per day.

When the weather began relenting in March she started walking every day with her pack. In the beginning she limited the walks to seven or eight miles and gradually increased the distance to fifteen. By the middle of April Melinda could easily cover twenty miles with a full pack. She even walked to Rockwell City twice. This was a round trip of thirty miles. She was tired after those walks but not unduly so. Deciding that she was prepared as she could possibly be, Melinda decided she would leave on the twentieth of April. She did what she could to prepare the place for being left empty. She turned off all the water and drained the systems. If it happened that she returned she didn't want to find frozen and ruptured water lines.

On the chosen morning Melinda shouldered her pack, snapped the leash on Maggie and they headed west. She was misty eyed as they departed. This had been a comfortable haven for almost three years and she had no idea what the future might hold. She resolutely turned west and Sac City was soon behind them. After they were clear of the town Maggie was released from the leash. They made good time and bedded down under an overpass where a state road ended at US 20. She had determined she was not going to cook unless she was inside with a stove. Melinda had packed two dozen energy bars in anticipation of a cold camp and two of these made up her meal that evening. They covered twenty-five miles the second day and spent the night in Correctionville in a small motel at the edge of town. There had been a major fire here and most of the business area of the town had been destroyed. Another long day took them to the outskirts of Sioux City where they again found a motel which had lights plus hot water thanks to a still functioning solar array.

It took most of the next day to get through the tangle of wrecked vehicles in Sioux City but by 4:00 pm they had crossed the state line and were in South Dakota. Melinda wept when she saw the first South Dakota highway sign. She still had many miles to travel but she felt she was almost home. They spent the night in the little town of Jefferson just off the freeway. They had been on the road for five days but it seemed much longer. Melinda found a comfortable room in the back of a roadside store. She shot a cottontail rabbit from in front of the store and opened canned fruit and vegetables from the storekeeper's pantry. The canned food tasted of age but it was still palatable. The gas stove was still working so she had a pleasant meal. Maggie even got to share as she was given some of the rabbit. Melinda decided she was going to stay over the next day and just rest. It was just as well she had made that decision because the next morning it was raining. It was a steady drizzle which continued all day and it would have been miserable walking in it. The mile markers on the map indicated that it was about seventy-five miles to the intersection of US 29 and US 90 just north of Sioux Falls. Melinda determined she was going to cover that distance in three days. On April 26 she set off with great determination and late in the day on April 28 her goal was in sight. Tired but pleased with her progress she bedded down under the overpass where the two highways crossed. Her meal that night were two of the energy bars. Every store seemed to have them on the shelf and though they tasted stale and dry they still seemed to provide the promised energy. After spending a night on the ground Melinda resolved to walk shorter days and spend more time looking for shelter. She spent five days covering the one hundred four miles to Watertown but she did manage to find shelter every night. Melinda was aware that she was losing weight from her already slender body. Her ribs were becoming prominent and she had taken up two holes in her belt to prevent her hiking shorts from slipping off her hips.

From Watertown to the town of Seneca was a distance of one hundred forty miles. Melinda covered that distance in seven days. She chose to rest for a day before undertaking the final push to Eagle Butte which was another ninety miles or so. Eagle Butte was where she expected to find some of her people if any of them had survived. Melinda found a house with no bodies inside and a working gas stove in the kitchen. There were chickens running wild in the neighborhood so she promptly shot three of them. She cut them up and boiled them then sealed the pieces I plastic bags and hoped the meat would not spoil in the three days she would spend on the road. She was now in territory with which she was familiar. The urge to complete the trek became stronger with every passing hour. She didn't sleep well that night and was on the road before sunrise. She camped that night at the intersection of US 83 and the following day took her to the small town of La Plant. Melinda was now close enough that she was tempted to continue walking. For a number of reasons she decided walking through the night was not a good idea. She was tired and Maggie was exhausted. Every time they paused Maggie plopped to the ground to rest. They spent the night in the back room of a little gas station store. It was a place she had been in many times. She fondly remembered the elderly couple who had been the proprietors. They had always had a small candy or home baked cookie for any child who didn't have the few cents needed to purchase a treat.

Melinda dreamed that night of her childhood in Green Grass. The most vivid part of her dream was walking along the bank of the Moreau river holding hands with Brad at age twelve and walking the same path two years later when he first worked up the courage to kiss her. She also remembered asking him what had taken him so long to do so. She woke in the morning anxious to be on the road while at the same time fearful she would find no one in Eagle Butte.

The travelers were on the road at any early hour the next morning and made good time all day. In late afternoon they were approaching Parade and Melinda realized it was going to be late when they reached Eagle Butte. As the entered the town Melinda became aware of noises coming from the next block. They were sounds she had not heard in three years, voices, coming from six teen age boys playing with a soccer ball in the grass of a small park. The boys waved to her then stopped play and trotted over to the edge of the road and waited as she approached. One of the boys asked, "Who are you? I know everyone in town and you don't live here." Melinda removed her broad brimmed canvas hat and another of the boys spoke up. He said, "I know her, her name is Melinda, she was there when I was six and cut my ear really bad when we lived up at Green Grass. She took me to the clinic and held me in her lap while old Doc Smithers sewed it up. I think she cried more than I did and I cried at lot." By now Melinda was weeping openly. One of the first of her people she had met was someone with whom she had a personal tie. The boy's name was Michael Stanley and she remembered him very well. This group of people was disturbing to Maggie. She took a defensive stance in front of Melinda and the hair on her neck and back was erect. One of the boys laughed and commented that she sure looked fierce for such a little thing. Melinda calmed Maggie and had her smell each of the boys' hands and after that plus a few head pats Maggie ignored them all and plopped down in the grass to rest.

Michael insisted that Melinda must go home with him. His mother, Marjorie, knew Melinda well and had wondered aloud several times whether Melinda had survived in Chicago where she had gone to study medicine.

The two women had a happy but tearful reunion. Marjorie then sent Michael to pass the news to the other residents and invite them to come and welcome Melinda home. She then explained that there were only eight families living in Parade. Three of the boys who were with Michael were visiting from Eagle Butte and would go home on the school bus the next morning. Melinda explained that she should get back on the road to be in Eagle Butte by dark. Marjorie suggested she stay overnight and ride the bus the next morning. The families gathered and it was soon decided to have a welcome home potluck to celebrate Melinda's return. As it turned out Melinda knew six of the eight families and they spent the evening speaking of the old days plus the events which had transpired since the day of the Death Star which was how the Cheyenne people referred to the event. Melinda was almost overwhelmed by the number of voices but she was happy to the point of tears to hear them. Maggie was beside herself with the joy of having a half dozen children to play with. The woman and the dog both went to sleep that night happy and contented with the new world with people in it.

After a leisurely breakfast with Marjorie and her family next morning Melinda got on the bus, really a large van, for the short drive to Eagle Butte. She was dropped off at the home of her uncle, Gray Eagle. He had been informed of her arrival last evening so her appearance was not a surprise to him. She was greeted warmly and Gray Eagle insisted she was to live with him and his wife. They had a large house and their children were all grown and living on their own, Melinda's mother had been killed in an auto accident before she moved to Chicago and she had no other living relatives.

Over the next ten days there was a steady stream of visitors who came to welcome Melinda home. There were four doctors in Eagle Butte who were operating a small clinic and hospital. They invited Melinda to join their practice with the promise of long hours, a lot of satisfaction and very little remuneration. They were paid with food and labor and the occasional gold nugget gleaned from the Black Hills by young men with a wanderlust.

Melinda fell into a routine of working five days at the clinic with two days spent becoming acquainted with her people again. She spent much time sewing for herself and others and even gave thought to walking to Seattle to search for Brad. It would be a daunting trek and she was frankly afraid of trying to travel that far alone with no assurance she would find Brad if she completed the trip.

The years passed and in 2114 the tribe set off on the migration to New Mexico. In Wyoming she met Chris and the rest of the story was well known to him.

Chapter 7 2156

Melinda's story only added to the admiration which Chris had felt for her for many years. Chris was tired, he leaned back in his chair and dozed for an hour. When he wakened he noted the time and was surprised that Carol had not appeared from the house. He went inside and found her on the living room sofa. Chris tried to waken Carol but she was totally unresponsive. He immediately called the emergency clinic, then called Kathie whom Carol always insisted was her primary physician. Kathie and the aid crew arrived almost simultaneously. Chris had called Brendon and Melinda so the Sweets and Hintzs were there also. Kathie asked Melinda to assist her and they finally concluded that Carol had suffered a massive stroke and there was little chance of a recovery. It was decided to leave her at home in her own bed rather than transport her to the hospital. An oxygen mask was put on her to aid her labored breathing. Chris insisted a chair be placed beside the bed and he sat there holding Carol's hand through the night. At a little after seven the next morning Carol opened her eyes, took a long shuddering breath, squeezed Chris's hand twice and passed away. Chris continued to hold Carol's hand until Linda Ann took his arm and helped him from the room. She led him to the kitchen and served him coffee, toast and scrambled eggs.

Chris was surprised to discover that he was hungry until he realized he had not eaten anything for twenty hours. After he finished eating Chris refilled his coffee and told the group he wanted to be alone for a while. He told them he was going out to Carol's grove and meditate for a while. Carol's grove was a small half circle of ten hickory trees which opened to a view out over the river. Years ago they had built several seats which gave them a view of the bottom land and the river. This had been Carol's most favored spot in the world. She had spent countless hours here considering her blessings and contemplating the problems facing her family. Chris chose a double swing seat where he and Carol had often sat together, holding hands, while discussing whatever topic was important that day. He spent two hours alone in the grove with his thoughts, recalling the many memorable events of their life together. There were several bouts of quiet weeping as he considered the loss of the wonderful woman who had been his constant and loving companion for forty-two years.

Returning to the house Chris found everyone gone except his four children, Brendon and Phoebe. Kathie and Linda Ann had bathed Carol, brushed her hair and dressed her in what had been her favorite outfit. Chris Jr. told Chris that if it was alright with him they would like to have a memorial service for Carol at 10:00 am the next morning. They would attempt to notify the community and hold the service at the picnic shelter. Cremation would follow the service. Final placement of the ashes was a decision for Chris to make.

At the service the next day people were invited to speak of their memories of Carol. There were many who spoke. Some talked of the relationship to Carol in her capacity as a doctor. Others related stories of Carol's character as a caring and generous human being. All of Carol's children spoke of their memories of a loving mother and friend. Chris attempted to speak but he was overcome with emotion and was unable to continue. He was escorted back to his seat by Craig and Linda Ann who remained by his side the remainder of the service.

After the service all of the people of Wolf Song community gathered at Chris' home. Mavis had passed the word that there would be a Wolf Song supper that evening. Chris Jr. and Brendon Jr had put two large beef roasts and two hams on the grill and the women had decided who was to bring which side dishes. By five pm over forty people had gathered and at six they sat down to eat. Billie Brown took over as master of ceremonies. He invited anyone who wished to do so to speak. Chris was the first to ask for the microphone. He apologized for not speaking at the memorial service then told them what he had in mind for Carol's ashes. He was going to ask George and Martha to design and build a stone mausoleum large enough to hold his and Carol's ashes. It would be erected in Carol's grove facing out over the river. Chris thanked them all for coming then took his seat. Phoebe spoke next. She directed her remarks to Chris. Phoebe said they had experienced so many events and traveled so many mile with Chris and Carol that she and Brendon would be pleased if their ashes could be placed beside their cousin and best friend. Melinda followed with the same request then Billie Brown asked if his parents' ashes could be included. Chris said yes to all of them. By the time they finished eating George had completed a rough sketch of a low rock wall with niches for the urns and flat on top so visitors could sit and if they wished, talk with the departed occupants. They didn't know it at the time of course, but over the years this little memorial would grow to a fifteen acre memorial garden holding the remains of people who had been among the original settlers of the new Iowa.

The twin daughters of Mavis and Jonathon announced that if Uncle Chris didn't object they wanted to move in with him and stay until he felt he was ready to face living alone. Chris wasn't sure if this would work but agreed to give the arrangement a trial.

The young women, they were twenty-nine that summer, moved in and took the second floor bedroom holding twin beds. They owned and operated a small shop which dealt in art objects and handmade leather goods. Maggie had become a skilled portrait artist whose work was in demand and Meggie was known for leather goods, a skill she had learned from Doreen Wilhelm. They took turns tending the store so one of them was always at home with Chris. In the beginning Chris was ill at ease having someone other than Carol sharing the house. He soon began to enjoy the laughing voices and the fact that they were both excellent cooks did much to help him adjust to their presence. There was a steady stream of visitors to the house. One of his children or grandchildren were there every day. Both Kathie and Linda Ann looked and sounded so much like Carol that at times Chris found himself weeping after a visit. Chris so treasured the time with them he refused to answer the phone when either of them was present. Chris knew he shouldn't play favorites with his grandchildren but it was easier said than done. Dallon who was seventeen and had graduated from high school would enter the university in September. Dallon was one of his frequent visitors. The boy never tired of hearing the stories of the epic walks and solo flights Chris had made back in those first dark days when he was totally alone. Chris wasn't aware but Dallon was secretly recording every word with the idea of putting the stories into book form.

One day in August Chris asked Dallon if he had ever considered becoming a pilot. Dallon replied, "I think about it all of the time but school takes up almost every minute of my day." Chris related to Dallon that when he was the age of Dallon his own grandfather John had paid for flying lessons and given him a plane of his own. Chris continued by saying if he could select the instructor and choose the aircraft he would do the same for Dallon. They only stipulation Chris placed on the agreement was that Dallon must schedule ten hours per week to devote to flying. By the middle of August Dallon had soloed and in fact had accumulated twenty-five hours of solo flight time in a single engine aircraft. Chris had gone to Wichita and placed an order for the latest model twin engine jet. It would be several months before it would be ready for delivery so Chris arranged for lessons in a twin jet based in Perry.

In August Chris convinced Meggie and Maggie that he was ready to live by himself again and that it was time for them to return to the house they shared in New Home. With the young women gone the house at first, felt empty and forlorn. As that first day wore on Chris began to feel Carol's presence. When he sat in her favorite chair he was comforted with the feeling that she was still with him and would be so until the end of his days. He brought the urn containing Carol's ashes and placed it on the mantle directly below her picture. That night Chris slept sound-ly through the entire night and awakened feeling refreshed and ready to face the world again.

Chapter 8 2156

By October, George and Martha's crew had finished the memorial wall. They had also landscaped the area in front of the wall and put in an extensive lawn and several additional seats facing the river. Chris considered whether to have a family gathering when Carol's ashes were placed in the wall. In the end he decided to keep the urn in the house until his own death then have his and Carol's urns placed in the wall at the same time. He still drew some comfort in having Carol's remains in the house with him.

It had now been four months since Chris had taken an interest in his home and property. After inspecting the buildings and grounds he hired a crew to paint and make minor repairs as needed plus a landscaping company to restore the lawn and shrubbery in which Carol had always taken great pride. He refurbished all of the bird feeders and put up several new ones then made sure they remained well stocked with various kinds of bird food. He was rewarded with the pleasant sounds of the many birds talking or squabbling over a place to perch while eating.

Chris decided it was time to revisit the accounts of Brendon and Phoebe and their stories of the first days following the day of the Red Star.

Chapter 9 2106

Brendon awoke at noon. He had arrived at his apartment at 6:00 am that morning after working a twenty hour shift at the potato processing plant in Gooding, Idaho.

There had been problems with the machines processing potatoes for both shredded and French fried varieties. As plant engineer he had felt compelled to stay with his crew until the problems were resolved. Brendon had been on the job for a year and a half after graduating from WSU at age twenty-one. He was young for his position but the plant superintendent cared only about results and Brendon provided those.

On awakening Brendon's first thought was to reflect on the absolute quiet. He had left the screened windows open to catch the morning breeze and there should have been traffic noise from the nearby highway. Looking outside he could not see a single moving vehicle or person on foot. He showered again took his time over breakfast then prepared to return to the plant. When he stepped out of his door he immediately became aware of two people lying on the floor in front of the elevator. Upon checking he discovered they were both dead and that the bodies were cool to the touch. Going back to his apartment Brendon tried to call the apartment manager's office. There was no answer until the answering machine clicked on. Brendon went back to the elevator which, when it answered the call button, opened to show three more bodies inside.

Brendon, in shock, took the stairs three floors to the lobby where he found more of what he had witnessed upstairs. There were at least a half dozen bodies including the manager who was sitting slumped over with her head and shoulders on her desk.

There were no signs of trauma or violence on any of the bodies. It was as if all of them had simply stopped living at the same time. Brendon was puzzled and more than a little panicked. What he was seeing just didn't seem possible. He walked out to the street only to have his fears multiplied. There were bodies everywhere plus automobiles which had crashed into each other or into building fronts. There were even a few which were simply stopped in the middle of the street.

Brendon retrieved his small truck from the apartment parking area with the intention of looking around the small city. It soon became apparent that the devastation was city wide. In places there were so many stalled and wrecked vehicles he was forced to reverse his course. Brendon eventually drove to the potato processing plant where, upon entering, he found machinery still running with no one attending it. There were bodies lying all about including several which had fallen into running machinery and been badly mangled.

Brendon entered the control room and turned off all power and water then prepared to leave. There were too many bodies for one individual to deal with even though some were close friends with whom he had worked every day. Returning to his apartment Brendon sank into his favorite chair and contemplated his future. One thing was certain. He would have to move. In a few days the stench of decaying bodies would render the apartment unlivable. After considering his options he decided returning home made the most sense. Home was central Washington State where most of his immediate family was engaged in farming and raising cattle. He would start out driving. His small truck was a hybrid capable of covering six hundred miles with a fully charged battery and a full tank of diesel fuel. With the possibility that he would not be able to find fuel or a working charging station Brendon concluded he should travel light. In the eventuality that he was forced to start walking he wanted to be able to carry everything comfortably in his hiking pack. He stowed all of his camping gear in the back of the truck which was fitted with a canopy. With his back pack filled with clothing and toiletries he was ready for the highway.

Brendon spent that night in his apartment. He didn't sleep well and was up, showered and dressed by five the next morning. He was not hungry but forced himself to eat two toaster waffles. He spent an hour driving around Gooding on the chance of finding survivors he had missed the day before. Again finding no people he drove onto US 84 and headed west. He drove at a moderate speed and carefully scanned the many vehicles which were wrecked or merely stopped on the highway. When he approached Boise in late afternoon he was forced to slow to a very low speed. The highway was literally clogged with wrecked vehicles. In two places there had been fires following the collisions and in one of them the goods in a semi-trailer were still smoldering.

At Caldwell he exited the highway to look for a place to spend the night. He found a motel with a convenience store next door with lights burning in both places. The first room Brendon checked was unlocked and ready for the next guests. He drove next door where he filled his fuel tank and even found a five gallon can with a spout. He filled it with diesel and placed it in the back of the truck where he secured it in place with bungee cords. Going into the store Brendon found a plentiful supply of food. The fresh produce was badly wilted but there was enough canned staples that he decided to take enough to last him all of the way home. He estimated it would take no more than two and a half or three days to get to the home of his parents just outside Ephrata. He boxed up enough food for twice that amount of time and stowed it in the truck.

Returning to the motel he plugged the truck's charging cord into the outlet outside his room and was relieved when the indicator showed the battery was being charged. Brendon checked the plumbing and was rewarded with hot water. After shaving he took a long hot shower and put on clean clothing. There was a small washer and dryer in his room so he used those to launder what he had been wearing for three days. He ate his supper right out of the cans without heating it. He was joined at his meal by two cats and a small dog. He dumped what was left from the cans on the sidewalk and all three animals went after it as though starved. On a whim Brendon went into the manager's apartment where he soon found both dog and cat food plus food and water dishes. Setting the dishes out on the walk he filled them with food and water then watched in satisfaction as the animals tried to make up for not have eaten for three or four days.

Brendon slept well that night and was on the road by six am. He had fed the animals again and propped his room door open so they could escape bad weather. He didn't hold much hope for their future but it was about all he could do for them.

Brendon made good time that day. There were fewer wrecked cars to contend with. The terrain wasn't flat but the grades and curves were gentle and it made for a pleasant drive if one could forget the reason for making it. Just south of La Grande all of that changed. When Brendon saw the sign for a rest area he suddenly became aware that he needed to answer the call of nature. Brendon rolled to a stop in front of the restroom building. When he looked up he became aware of three people wrestling or indulging in horseplay beside a covered picnic table. There was a young woman and two men. The woman and one of the men, who appeared to be a middle aged and quite heavy individual' and were both naked. Brendon almost started the truck to drive on but changed his mind. He had stopped because he needed to use the restroom and he was going to do so As he got out of the truck he picked up the eleven mm Smith and Wesson from the center console and tucked it under his belt.

Brendon was going to have to pass within fifteen feet of the trio to reach the restroom. As he approached he could see the naked man mopping at his face with a bloody undershirt. The second man was grasping the woman's arms in an effort to control her. Brendon could see scratches on both of her arms and across her abdomen. Brendon stopped and the woman, who was not much more than a girl, said, "Mister will you help me?" At this point the man who was holding the woman addressed Brendon. He said, "You need to stay out of this and just go on up the road. We chased this girl for three days and now she belongs to us." Brendon replied that it didn't appear as if the woman was anxious to belong to anyone and perhaps she should be released. The man replied, "I won't tell you again, get in your truck and leave." Brendon said, "I can't in good conscience do that, you need to release her and step away before this escalates any further."

The man released the woman's arms then backhanded her across the face. At the same time the woman delivered a solid kick to his lower shin. She was weary sturdy hiking boots so it was a painful blow. The man staggered back a couple of steps then pulled a wicked looking hunting knife from his belt and started to charge at Brendon. By now Brendon had the pistol in his hand. He held fire until the man was no more than seven or eight feet away. Brendon fired two rounds into the center of the man's chest. The two heavy slugs stopped him in his tracks and knocked him over onto his back. Brendon swung the pistol to cover the naked man who was staring blankly at the scene in front of him while blood continued to leak from his nose and mouth. After checking and determining that the man on the ground was dead Brendon turned to the second man and told him to get dressed.

While waiting for the man to dress Brendon turned to the woman and asked her name. "Phoebe," she replied, "Phoebe Jane McGuire." Brendon then said, "Phoebe it is apparent that being naked doesn't present a problem for you, however I must confess that it is very disconcerting to me. Why don't you find your clothing and get dressed?" Phoebe who was suddenly blushing a deep red all the way down to her shoulders replied that her clothing had been ripped and cut off and most likely was not wearable. She added that she had been so angry and frightened she had forgotten about her nakedness. She had abandoned her pack the day before in an effort to travel faster so she had nothing to put on. Brendon told her to go to his truck where she would find his pack containing a shirt, hiking shorts and new jockey shorts. They could use a piece of rope for a belt and safety pins to keep the underwear in place. He also asked her to bring his rifle which was in a gun rack in the cab.

While he waited for Phoebe to get dressed and return, Brendon pondered on what to do with his prisoner. There was no police agency where he could be delivered so that was not an option.

He considered just killing the man but knew he was not capable of a cold blooded execution. About the time he settled on what he would do, Phoebe returned with the rifle. She looked rather comical in an oversized shirt and hiking shorts but at least now Brendon could look at her without being embarrassed.

Brendon accepted the rifle from Phoebe then walked over to the table where the man sat, still mopping his face with the blood stained undershirt. Brendon abruptly asked the man, "How fast can you run?" The man replied, "Not very fast, what difference does it make?" Brendon told him he was going to get a chance which had not been offered to Phoebe. Brendon said he would give the man three minutes to run as far and fast as he could manage. If he was still in rifle range Brendon would shoot him. If not, he was free. Brendon then warned the man to go south if he escaped. Brendon was heading north and if he ever saw the man again he would kill him on sight. Brendon pulled a watch from his pocket and said, "Your three minutes start now," as he pushed a button. The man protested the he had no food or water and Brendon told him he used twenty seconds of his three minutes. The man took off in a shambling run while Brendon sat on the table with the rifle resting across his knees. Near the entrance the man stopped and moved to the driver's side door of a small truck. Brendon fired a round through the windshield of the vehicle and shouted, "Run." Phoebe had joined Brendon on the table. They watched the man continue on to the entrance ramp where he slowed, took a few stumbling steps then stopped. He clutched at his chest, slowly collapsed to the ground then rolled onto his back and was still. They watched for a few moments then walked out to where the man lay. He was lying with his eyes and mouth open but was not breathing. After observing the body for a few minutes Brendon commented that now they would not have to observe their back trail. They left the body where it had fallen and walked back to the visitor center building. Brendon's bladder was giving him sharp reminders of why he had stopped at the rest area. When that problem had been taken care of Brendon suggested they drive the short distance to La Grande. They should have time to find a motel and stores so Phoebe could replace her pack, clothing and other necessities needed by every woman whether at home or traveling.

It was dusk when they drove into La Grande. It was late because they had stopped to make and consume sandwiches. They found a motor court on the edge of the business district. The court was made up of ten cottages and a small office building. The first cottage they checked was unlocked and ready for the next occupants. Even better it was a two bedroom affair and even had separate bathrooms. There were bodies lying around outside but none in their rooms or in the manager's office or apartment. The bodies were beginning to smell of death so they closed the door and used a liberal amount of bathroom spray. Brendon knew that in a few days the place would be uninhabitable.

Phoebe sat down and began to compile a list of what she would need to acquire on her "shopping" trip the next morning. When they were ready to retire Brendon offered Phoebe a white cotton undershirt for sleep wear and she asked if she could use his tooth brush as she had none. After going to bed Brendon tossed and turned for some time. His mind was racing with thoughts of the many decisions and options he would be facing in the next days and weeks. Not the least of these was what to do about the young woman sleeping in the next room. As he was finally dropping off to sleep Brendon was fully awakened when Phoebe slipped into the bed and snuggled up to his back. Brendon, startled, said "What" and started to turn over. Phoebe pushed him back down then said, "Go back to sleep, we will talk in the morning. I just don't want to be alone tonight." Brendon slept well through the remainder of the night but at the same time was acutely aware of the warm body beside him in the bed.

When Brendon awoke he was alone in the bed. Phoebe was not in either room so he took his time shaving and showering. He dressed in the first clean clothing he had put on in three days and went out to meet the day. He found Phoebe sitting in the shade of a cottonwood tree with a cup of coffee. Phoebe jumped up, gave him a demure kiss on the cheek and said, "Good morning my hero." She then told him to have a seat and she would bring him coffee and a breakfast sandwich. She was back in less than three minutes with a large mug of coffee and two sausage and egg sandwiches. In response to Brendon's questioning look she told him the place formerly served breakfast and had a large, well-stocked freezer.

While Brendon was eating Phoebe told him she had a speech to make. Brendon nodded and Phoebe began speaking. She said, "I believe we are fated to be together. I think that is why you arrived when you did yesterday and why events occurred as they did. I want to be with you through whatever the future holds. I want to bear your children and hold your hand when you are old and ill, however; I will not live with you as man and wife unless we are married. If you do not want to do this we can part amicably today and I will find a vehicle and start for Bend where my family was until the end came last week. I doubt if they survived but it was home and a place to start over." Brendon could only sit with his mouth open and stare at this young woman who continued to amaze him. Phoebe broke the silence by saying, "I believe the ball is now in your court Mr. Hintz, now let's go shopping."

They drove to the center of the business district and parked. Phoebe told him that she didn't need help with her shopping but that while Brendon was waiting for her she would be pleased if Brendon would find a compact twenty-two caliber pistol and a small bore hunting rifle for her. She wanted one which would put down a deer sized animal or if need be a man. She told him she had no intention of ever again being forced to run from people such as the two cretins who had pursued her for the better part of three days.

It took Phoebe three hours to obtain all of the items on her list. It took Brendon less than half of that to complete his. He found a gun shop and picked out a Colt semi-automatic pistol. He also found a light weight rifle chambered for the 223 Winchester cartridge. Brendon returned to the truck and put the weapons and a plentiful supply of ammunition behind the seat. He picked up a pen and writing pad and went to sit under an umbrella in front of an outdoor café. Not being sure what he wanted to write he made several attempts and finally ended up with a simple document with the heading Certificate of Marriage. The body of the statement simply said, "We the undersigned, Brendon Helmut Hintz and Phoebe Jane McGuire declare that we are married. We both promise to be faithful to our spouse, to work hard at our marriage and to show respect for each other. We do not promise to always be obedient as that is not the character of either of us." Brendon read the paper several times then signed and date it April 16, 2106. When Phoebe returned to the truck she was laboring under the weight of two huge shopping bags plus a backpack which she had slung over one shoulder. Brendon helped her stow her acquisitions in the back of the truck then suggested they drive to Pendleton before stopping for the night. From Pendleton they could easily drive to the home of his parents in one day. Phoebe agreed and they were soon north bound on US 84. Brendon picked the note pad up from the dash and handed it to Phoebe. He said, "Read this and if you want to make changes, feel free to do so."

Phoebe read the page then she read it again. She said, "This is perfect, we don't need to change a word." She then asked to use Brendon's pen and signed the paper with a flourish. When they stopped to stretch their legs in mid-afternoon Phoebe walked to Brendon's side of the truck. She embraced him and lifting her face to his she said, "Mr. Hintz you may kiss your bride." When they stepped away from each other Brendon made the comment that he had been kissed before but now he had been kissed permanently.

They drove into Pendleton in late afternoon and found a solar powered motel with a room made up and ready for guests.

They ate little and slept less that night. However they were up and ready to travel at sunrise. The truck was fueled and their breakfast was microwaved sandwiches. By the middle of the morning they had crossed the Columbia and were approaching Kennewick. After passing through Kennewick then Pasco they headed north on US 395. At the intersection where Washington route 17 split off to go north to Moses Lake they encountered the greatest surprise of their journey. Parked on the shoulder of the road was a camper van. Behind the van, sitting at a small table under a beach umbrella were two people.

Brendon pulled over and parked the truck behind the van. As a precaution he loosened his pistol in the holster and unsnapped the restraining strap. He was not overly concerned but after their recent experience he was taking no chances. Brendon quickly saw the two people were an elderly couple of perhaps seventy-five or eighty years of age. The man stepped forward with his hand extended. He said, "My name is Calvin Campbell and this lady is my wife Carolyn. We are Helpers, I am guessing that you are Brendon Hintz and you are on your way home." Brendon could only stare at the man in amazement but finally managed to say, "That is correct, but how did you know and what is a Helper?" Brendon introduced Phoebe as his wife and asked Calvin if he had an explanation of what had happened.

Calvin explained that the full explanation was rather lengthy and would be given in detail when the travelers reached their programmed destination. For Brendon that was Mount Vernon, Washington. For Phoebe, since she was not on his list, it meant southern California. Calvin told them the programmed destinations were not mandatory but had been chosen based on the location of the individual at the time they were chosen. They had been picked by a random computer selection and then had been inoculated against an airborne virus which eventually wiped out the vast majority of mankind. A small transceiver had been implanted which was intended to draw them to their assigned destination. He then asked if the birthmarks they had on their right hip had been itching since the day the earth died. When both Phoebe and Brendon said yes, Calvin told them it was an indication the homing transceiver was working. When they arrived in Mount Vernon the unit would be turned off using an electronic wand. Eventually, it would work to the surface of the skin and fall off. The birthmark which was actually an antenna grown by the body would remain with them for life. Calvin pointed out that less the one person in ten thousand had received the inoculation plus the homing device. Of that number there had been suicides and deaths from accidents. Currently there were less than thirty thousand people alive in the U.S.

As for being a Helper there were twenty-five pairs of people who were stationed across the country to help the confused survivors find their way to one of the two chosen areas. To his knowledge Calvin and Carolyn were the only married couple known to have survived. Most of the Helpers were older people less able to cope with the physical labor involved in creating new communities.

The two couples decided to see if they could find a suitable place to spend the night in the little village of Mesa then go their separate ways in the morning. Brendon and Phoebe would go north to Moses Lake while Calvin and Carolyn would take US 395 northeast to I-90 then east to the Spokane area to spend a month searching for survivors.

They found a small house with no bodies just off the main street and spent a pleasant evening around a fire pit in the back yard. In the morning the older couple were on the road early as they had a good distance to travel. Brendon and Phoebe lingered over their coffee and started out a little after nine. Phoebe, not knowing she would see another woman with whom she could converse, wept when the Campbell's pulled out onto the highway.

The forty mile drive to Moses Lake went quickly. Brendon, knowing what he was going to find at home, was tense and short with words when he spoke at all. They drove through Moses Lake then took a county road which led to the farm. The farm was a family enterprise with both of Brendon's brothers plus a sister and her husband involved. They farmed six full sections of land which were all adjacent. The four houses Brendon needed to visit were located within two miles of each other.

Brendon turned into the long driveway heading to the parking area behind his parent's home. Before they arrived at the parking area the smell of death became more and more pronounced. As they parked the truck and exited the vehicle the odor was overpowering. They entered the back yard to find Brendon's entire family strewn about. The eight adults appeared to have been seated on the patio while the three children were on the lawn nearby. Brendon could only stand and stare at the scene. Phoebe burst into tears. She had not known these people but through Brendon she felt a strong bond with them. Brendon finally spoke. He said, "I can't leave them like this, I have to bury them."

They went into the house and gathered enough blankets to wrap all of the bodies. From the machine shed Brendon brought a spool of bailing twine. Wrapping the bodies was an ordeal with both them retching more or less constantly from the terrible odor. When the task was completed Brendon attached a back hoe to a tractor and began excavating a grave. It became dark before he finished the grave. In spite of the smell they spent the night in the home of the elder Hintz's and resumed work on the grave in the morning. By noon the task was finished and the grave covered.

They drove to the home of Brendon's youngest brother. Before entering the house Brendon removed every article of his clothing and Phoebe did the same. The clothing went into a gas fueled incinerator and was soon converted to ashes. They then went into the house where they got into separate showers and scrubbed until the water ran cold. They put on clothing belonging to Brendon's brother and sister-in-law. The clothing didn't exactly fit but it would do until they could replace it. Brendon was convinced the odor from his parents' home had permeated the interior of his truck. He unloaded the truck and discarded everything he thought was capable of absorbing the odor. Feeling that the smell had seeped into the upholstery of the truck cab Brendon decided to leave it and take a near new nine passenger van parked in his brother's garage.

They left the farm and drove into Ephrata which was a ghost town. There were many bodies on the streets and in some area scattered bones. They saw numerous coyotes and assumed they had gathered to take advantage of the plentiful source of food. It had been less than a month but the wild canines had soon realized there was no longer a threat from man.

Brendon decided they would drive to Wenatchee where there were more stores from which to choose to replace their clothing and the other articles they had discarded. They would spend the night in Wenatchee then drive to Mount Vernon the next day.

Highway 2 had been widened to four lanes several years ago and the trip across Stevens Pass was no longer the arduous trek it had been in the past.

They arrived in Wenatchee in late morning and were soon "shopping." Both of them picked up more articles than they had discarded. They even picked up a supply of winter clothing. The back seats of the van were piled high with clothing and shopping bags. They had discussed the situation and thought they could find everything they needed in Mount Vernon. However they decided to take care of their needs where the goods were at hand rather than risk not being able to find them later. Both of them felt a pang of guilt at just walking in and taking things but there was no alternative. They completed their shopping and decided to travel on before stopping for the night. They drove at a low speed as there were numerous cars stopped or wrecked on the highway. The odor as they passed told them which ones contained bodies. They were forced to drive through parking lots and on side streets to get through Leavenworth. Some sort of festival had been in progress and the highway was a tangled mass of vehicles.

When they crossed Stevens Pass there was still a heavy blanket of snow at the top of the ski areas. From the number of cars in the parking lots it appeared as if they had still been operating when the end came.

They stopped in the little town of Skykomish and after searching found a motel cabin with no bodies in it or close enough to be a problem. Their supper that night was from cans they had picked up in Wenatchee. They slept that night to the soothing sound of the river tumbling over the rocks.

In the morning both Phoebe and Brendon were anxious to be on the road. They had a breakfast of leftovers from last night's supper and an energy bar. They started out with Phoebe driving and she drove with a heavy foot. The only problem they encountered was a tangled mass of cars on the east side of Monroe. Phoebe shifted the van into four wheeled drive then drove through the ditch, a couple of planting strips and two parking lots until they were back on the highway. When they arrived at the intersection with Interstate 5 in Everett, Phoebe suggested that Brendon drive the rest of the way.

The thirty mile trip to Mount Vernon went quickly. The highway had been cleared of wrecked and abandoned vehicles by simply pushing them into the ditches. As instructed by Calvin, Brendon took exit 227 and turned east on College Way. In two short blocks they saw the storefront sign which said, "Fabrics and Sewing Supplies."

As they parked and were getting out of the van a middle-aged couple walked out of the store and greeted them. The couple identified themselves as Jack Wilson and Martha Brown. They told the newcomers they would explain what had happened to the world and help them find a suitable home.

Brendon and Phoebe were taken to a store which had been converted to a dormitory. They were assigned a room which held two cots, a sink and a toilet. There were showers and laundry facilities across the hall. A kitchen and dining facility had been set up next door. The menu was limited but adequate. They were asked to come to the office at nine the next morning for a debriefing and orientation session. They brought their bags containing clothing and toiletry items to the room and Phoebe had Brendon help her move the cots until they were side by side against each other. She explained that she didn't get married to sleep across the room from her husband.

They went to the dining room at 5:30 pm and were surprised to find seven other people waiting to be served. All seven of them had arrived within the past three days. Their occupations had varied from attorney to nurse to a goldsmith/jeweler. There were also two grocers and two teachers who had been employed at the same school in eastern Montana. They asked permission then pushed three tables together and held a lively discussion during their meal. They talked about their lives prior to the "day" and the routes they had followed to Mount Vernon.

The next morning the nine newcomers met with Jack and Martha and were given the story of what had happened to their world. Jack gave them only a thumbnail sketch of the events but each person was given a packet of papers which presented the dates and known facts in detail. Jack told them a trickle of people were showing up almost every day and currently there were some two hundred twenty-five people in residence. Seventy-five of that number had moved on to Bellingham. There was a small medical clinic in each community and centers were being established in both cities where people could go for basic food commodities and clothing without having to resort to scavenging individual stores.

When asked what he wanted to do with his future Brendon replied that he had been born and reared as a farmer. He added that he could best contribute to the new society by resuming that activity. Phoebe spoke up and told them she saw her future in assisting her husband in whatever he chose to do.

After the meeting ended, Jack told the Hintz's he had something to show them if they had an hour or two to spare. At this point they had nothing but time so they followed Jack as he got on the freeway and headed south. Two miles south of Mount Vernon Jack left the highway and headed west. After a half mile he turned up a long driveway which led to a well-kept looking set of buildings including a huge old house. After parking and getting out of the vehicle Jack suggested they inspect the house first. He told them if the house failed to meet Phoebe's approval then looking at the rest of the farm would be a waste of time.

The house contained five bedrooms, four bathrooms and a large kitchen. There was a layer of dust everywhere but otherwise the place was clean and tidy. Phoebe was silent as they examined the place. There was a well-furnished living room plus a large dining room, a family room and an office. As they completed their tour and headed outside Phoebe finally spoke. She turned to Brendon and said, "If the rest of the place meets your approval then we are home." Brendon replied, "Then we are home, I will make the rest of the place work for us."

Phoebe and Brendon moved in that day and soon became prominent members of the growing community.

Chapter 10 2156

A fter Chris finished reading he poured a mug of coffee and sat contemplating what he should do next. He now had the accounts of five survivors although Phoebe's story was incomplete. He would ask Phoebe to fill in her experiences up to the time she had met Brendon. He would also locate five other survivors and ask them to write their stories of the first days following the day of death. When he had all ten accounts in hand he would contact a publisher and have them printed in book form. The book would be made available, free of charge, to anyone who wanted a copy. Chris felt it was important that the younger generations and the immigrants know what the survivors had endured following the day their world had ended.

That evening Chris was treated to an hour long rendition of wolf song. It sounded as if the full pack of years past had gathered and joined in the chorus. It reminded him of the many times he and Carol had sat on the deck holding hands while listening to the song of the wild canines. He wept a little and at the same time seemed to sense the presence of Carol. It gave him a feeling of peace and that night he had the first night of undisturbed sleep since her passing.

When Chris awoke the next morning his first thoughts concerned the question of which of the young people would stop by to check on him that day. Since Carol's death one of his children or others of their generation had visited him every single day. They brought him goodies, ran errands for him and helped with chores around the house and yard.

Today it was Billie Brown who arrived at a little after 8:00 am. They sat with coffee and discussed the mundane things of the

community and families. Chris mentioned the book he was going to have published from the stories of the survivors. He told
Billie the names of the stories he now had and said he wanted to
obtain five more to fill out the book. Billie immediately pointed
out that Chris already had Lisa Meyers account and added that
his father had maintained a diary all of his life and his story could
be gleaned from that source. Billie also suggested that Chris contact Doreen Wilhelm to see if she could provide information on
her late husband Hans. Doreen was now 84 but her mind was
still sharp and Billie was confident she knew enough of Hans's
history to provide an account of it. Next, Billie suggested that
perhaps the story of Lori's early life could be included. She was
not one of the survivors but her travels from birth to arrival in
New Home had been as long and convoluted as any of the actual
survivors.

After thinking about Billie's proposal Chris concluded that
with the nine stories he had enough material for the book. He
would not need to search any farther than New Home to obtain
what he needed to fill out the book.

Chapter 11 2158

It had now been two years since Carol's passing and Chris still missed her as much as he had in the beginning. Not a day passed without some event or object bringing her to mind. One of his or Brendon's children or grandchildren came by every day. The women and girls kept the house clean and tidy. The men and boys took care of the lawn and shrubbery.

The book which Chris had assembled was published and immediately became very popular. It was titled simply "Survivors." It was decided to charge a modest fee for the book. The income from the book would be used to maintain and expand the memorial garden on the hill behind the Weddle house. The population of survivors was aging and there were requests every week for a place in the garden. A new paved road and parking area had been built just to the west of the Weddle house. It enabled people to visit and park without intruding on the privacy of Chris and Billie Brown.

Chapter 12 2158

There were vast areas of the west and northwest which were unsettled or very thinly so. Disturbing news began to filter in from some of those areas.

Bands of armed men reminiscent of the late 1800's had formed and were robbing and harassing travelers and small communities. As yet no one had been killed but authorities felt it was only a matter of time until that occurred. Some of the gangs traveled by motor vehicle but most of them were mounted on horses. That mode of travel was slower but it enabled them to move off the roads. They could disappear into the vast stretches of prairie or mountains where no vehicle could conveniently travel.

The Justice Department was given the task of ending these depredations. The first step in the campaign as the operation was called was to print thousands of posters. The posters were plastered all over the areas in which the gangs were known to be operating. The posters simply stated that if the gang members surrendered all automatic weapons and returned to their homes by the end of October they would not be pursued or prosecuted.

Two companies of U.S. Marshal were being formed and trained. Their job, after October, would be to hunt down and arrest the robbers. Anyone who fired a weapon at or offered armed resistance to the marshals would be subject to the death penalty. This information was printed in every newspaper in the country and aired on every television station as well. The new satellites insured that the information could be seen everywhere in the country. The marshals had two new weapons which had not been made public.

Both weapons were aircraft. First was a small jet fighter. It was not very fast but it was whisper quiet. There were four 20 mm guns mounted in the nose. These guns were mounted in a new system which allowed them to be swept from side to side in a ten degree arc. The plane had soon been given the nickname the "Broom." The second aircraft was a helicopter. Due to a radical rotor re-design it was also ultra-quiet. The "Night Owl" as the helicopter was called was capable of carrying fifteen men plus their arms and equipment. It carried two 20 mm guns in a pod beneath the nose. These guns had the same sweeping mechanism as those on the "Broom."

By the end of October it appeared as if all of the gangs except three had surrendered their weapons and retired. The most active of the gangs was operating around Rapid City and using the vastness of the Black Hills and the Badlands to the east to escape and hide out after one of their raids.

It was decided the marshals would only deal with one gang at a time and that they would start with the Black Hills group. Accordingly, plans were made to move both troops of marshals, two helicopters and one of the "Brooms" to South Dakota. They would be located at the long abandoned Ellsworth AFB after a dormitory and dining facility had been put back into a usable condition.

Two days before the marshals and their gear were due to arrive the bandits struck. The choice of targets for the raid would always remain a mystery. Hermosa was a small village lying along the banks of a stream named Battle. There were less than fifty people living in the area and only three businesses. There was a store which sold clothing, a few food items plus farm and ranch supplies, a small café and a saloon.

There were seven members in the gang. All seven of them entered the store waving weapons which varied from pistols to automatic rifles. The store owner, a crusty old survivor of the dark days, ordered them out of the store and refused to open the cash drawer or the safe. He was beaten and then shot dead for his efforts. The gang, after prying open the till and rifling the dead man's pockets, had a total of $320 to show for their work. In a collective fit of anger they shot up the interior of the store then set it on fire. As they were leaving a local resident was taking pictures and he also was shot dead. Across the street a twelve year old girl was seen looking out a window. She was subjected to several bursts of automatic weapons fire. She was wounded by one round of the first burst but fell to the floor and the remaining bullets passed above her. The gang then boarded two vans and headed southwest towards what had been Custer State Park.

They had taken over what had been the Park Ranger's residence and had used it as a refuge and rest stop for the past two years. Their plan was to stay for two days then take saddle horses plus three with packs of supplies and proceed to the cabins they used for a winter home deep within the Black Hills.

Chapter 13 2158

The marshals arrived at Ellsworth and before they were unpacked they had been informed of the raid and murders in Hermosa. The bandits felt so secure in the park headquarters they stayed for three days. On the fourth day they saddled their horses, loaded three pack animals and proceeded west at a leisurely pace. They were not aware that the citizens of the Hermosa area, incensed over the wanton shootings, had kept them under close observation almost from the moment they had departed from the little town. The marshals had been alerted to the situation and by one pm ten officers in a helicopter were crossing the eastern boundary of the park. In support of the helicopter the "Broom" was circling the area at eighteen thousand feet. The plane was so quiet it could not be heard at ground level.

At perhaps a mile inside the west entrance to the park the chopper swept around a curve and there, stretched over 150 yards or so, were seven riders and three pack horses. The pilot made a low pass over the group then turned sharply and retraced his path. By the time the chopper started the second run the riders had their weapons in hand and were firing at the helicopter. The men inside could hear bullets impacting the armored floor of the aircraft. None of the rounds penetrated the cabin and in seconds the helicopter was clear and out of range. By this time the little jet fighter was down to three hundred feet and lined up behind the seven riders. They had cut the pack horses loose and were galloping desperately for the next curve which was no more than a quarter of a mile away. It may as well have been five miles. The pilot had his guns set to sweep and in one pass which lasted less than five seconds every one of the horses was hit and knocked off its feet. The riders fared no better.

When the helicopter carrying the marshals moved in and landed there was no one alive among the bandits. Surprisingly two of the outlaws turned out to be women. The bodies were searched for identification and many photos were taken to aid in that process. As had become the custom in dealing with the remains of deceased criminals, the bodies were stripped to their underwear and left beside the road at the mercy of the elements and scavengers. The dead horses were stripped of their gear and dragged to the side of the road as well.

The three pack horses were caught up, relieved of their packs and turned loose. After carefully searching the packs and the personal possessions of the bandits the marshals had a total of only $640 in cash. That didn't seem to be much for a band which had spent more than a year terrorizing the countryside.

The general opinion about the event was that by ending the way it had it would save the time and expense of a trial.

Chapter 14 2158

The next target of the marshals was to a group operating in the northwest area of Kansas. The location was a puzzle. There were no large population centers in that part of Kansas and robberies committed by the gang of five seldom netted them more than two or three hundred dollars. They operated around the little town of Goodland, hiding out in abandoned farms and ranches and for the most part moving about only at night.

The marshals planned to set up their base in Colby and use the helicopters to locate and eventually run the bandits to ground. There was a small local airport at Colby and while there were no landing lights or radar, the single grass runway was long enough for the "Broom" to land and take off.

As the marshals were organizing their move from South Dakota to Kansas the outlaw gang made a decision which obviated the need for the marshals to move to Kansas. The gang decided that rather than spend the winter hiding out in cold houses they would move. Their plan was to go west into Colorado and then south to the Lamar area where there was a sizable population. They would pass the winter in comfort and in the spring move east to the Garden City and Dodge City areas which should provide a greater return for their nefarious activities.

The gang loaded their clothing, weapons and a few household possessions into a nine passenger van and headed west on US 70. They planned to go west to Seibert then turn south towards Lamar. They were late getting started so it was lunch time when they entered the town of Burlington just a few miles into Colorado. They entered a small roadside diner and after eating were standing beside the van talking. One of the gang commented that the store across the street looked prosperous and seemed to be doing a brisk business. He added that perhaps they should relieve the store of any excess cash and fatten the bag holding their traveling money. The others readily agreed so they drove across the street and entered the store with drawn guns. The robbery was proceeding smoothly until a woman clerk began berating the robbers for what they were doing. Her tirade continued until she received a sharp slap across the face and was told to shut up. The slap set off a general melee. Eventually shots were fired and two clerks were wounded although neither wound was serious. The gang backed out of the store with guns still out, got in their van and headed west.

This area was part of Colorado which had been deeded to the Cheyenne people. The Cheyenne were sparsely settled over all of their territory but they had set up a phone network and every community checked in with tribal headquarters in Yuma every day.

Within minutes of the aborted robbery the two wounded clerks were in the local clinic having their wounds treated. A small plane had been sent up to locate the van and keep it under surveillance. The van was soon spotted and by circling a mile or so behind the van the plane was able to remain unseen by the robbers. At Seibert the van turned south and this fact was relayed to tribal authorities.

Over the telephone net it was discovered that a party of twelve men were seven or eight miles north of Kit Carson hunting buffalo to supplement their winter meat supply. The hunting party had two refrigerated trucks plus three other vehicles. In a short time the vehicles were moved out to the highway and used to create a rather substantial roadblock.

In mid-afternoon the van appeared over a low rise moving at a low rate of speed. It drove to within twenty-five yards of the roadblock and stopped. For perhaps 30 seconds there was no sound or movement in the van. Then the doors flew open and all five of the bandits piled out into the road firing their weapons more or less blindly. The hunters, each of whom had been chosen for his skill with a rifle, returned fire. The incident was over in seconds. All five of the bandits lay on the roadway, dead or dying.

By phone the hunters were instructed to search the bodies and van for anything which could be used for identification, take pictures of the bodies and then strip them and put them out in the field for the carrion eaters. Except for notifying the marshals and sending what ID information they had discovered the incident was considered closed.

Television and the print media flooded the county with the gruesome photos from the scenes of the demise of both gangs. The third gang which was due for the attention of the marshals had been operating in west Texas with their headquarters loosely based in Amarillo. After ten days of watching or reading of the destruction of the other two outlaw bands there was a change of heart about their chosen occupation. They ditched their vehicles, turned their horses loose and dumped their weapons down an abandoned well which was then filled with sand and rocks. One by one they began to straggle north or east to return to their former lives.

The marshal troops were disbanded but the individuals were assigned in pairs to specific locales, primarily in the sparsely populated west.

Chapter 15 2159

Ten years ago discussions had begun to occur about recognizing the survivors of 2106. In 2159 the U.S. Government created a panel within the Interior Department whose purpose was to locate and identify the survivors.

Offices were set up around the country to poll citizens and enter those who qualified on the list of survivors. The only requirements for being added to the list was to have the ever present brown mark on the hip or to have a notarized statement signed by two survivors. The statement simply stated that the person was known to be alive prior to April 7, 2106.

It was discovered that the survivors now totaled less than forty percent of the number estimated for 2106. The number was decreasing every day as the population aged.

The Bureau of Survivors asked for and was given permission to have the U.S. Mint coin a gold medallion depicting the death star on one side and the survivors name on the other. The medallion was to be interred with the recipient's ashes at the time of his or her death. The presentation of the medallions was a public affair which was accompanied by speeches, parades and much fanfare.

A few medallions were coined with the names of deceased people who had been instrumental in organizing the new county back in the dark days. Among these were Jack and Martha Wilson, Hans Wilhelm and Carol Janine Weddle of the New Home community.

Chapter 16 2160

At the February Wolf Song supper Lori announced that she was pregnant again. The birth was due to occur in July and for the second time she was carrying twins. Not to be outdone, Christopher and Carolyn made it known that they were also expecting with a due date in August.

When the congratulations for the two pregnancies had subsided Chris stood and when it became quiet announced that he also had news to share. He began by saying he was bored with his life. With the family businesses in capable hands of the next generation and with Carol gone he had nothing to do. In spite of daily visits from children and grandchildren the house always felt empty.

Chris went on to say that while there were uncounted thousands of acres of farmland in Iowa and the other mid-western states there seemed to be a revival of the old American desire to move west. South Dakota seemed to be a favored destination. Chris had quietly sent two men to investigate. They had reported that the area around Huron was drawing a number of would be settlers. The only drawback to the area was the lack of suitable housing. After fifty plus years of being abandoned those homes built prior to the "day" were beyond being rehabilitated.

Chris proposed moving to the Huron area and opening a new composite plant to provide construction materials for the newcomers. He had sworn Dallon to secrecy and Dallon had agreed to fly Chris wherever and whenever he needed to go. Dallon was just finishing his last term at the University in Ames. He would graduate with a degree in Manufacturing Engineering and would be considered for the position of President and Chief Operating

Engineer of the plant. He would be young for the job but he had a number of uncles and close family friends to assist him over the rough spots in the process.

Chris sat down to stunned silence. Predictably, Phoebe was the first to speak. With no preamble she addressed Chris, "Chris, I am happy you have found something to which you can devote your time and energy. I and many others have been concerned about you. Without Carol and without others to worry about you have become glum and listless. This project will be good for you. I have to ask however, why it had to be so far from home. You and Brendon have been joined at the hip for forty-six years. He can't get through the day without huddling with you at least twice to discuss events both large and small. He will be like a new puppy with you gone, underfoot and needing constant assurance that all is well. You have all heard me say I was never moving again. I am gruff and often bossy but I remember the circumstance of meeting Brendon plus the kindness and love he had shown me for fifty-four years. If you are moving to South Dakota so are the Hintz's."

There was an audible gasp from the group seated around the fireplace in the shelter house.

Before the stunned group could resume talking Melinda was on her feet. She said to the group, "I also owe Chris more than I can ever repay. He led me halfway across the country to find Brad. He and Brendon became the brothers I never had, plus Carol and Phoebe became my sisters. I am eighty years old and do not have many years left. I want to spend those years with my family so Brad and I will be making the trip to South Dakota with the others."

Now George and Martha came forward to claim the microphone. They had been huddled and talking since Chris had divulged his plans. Martha spoke for both of them. She addressed her first words to Phoebe. "Mom, when we arrived here we were no more than one step up from being feral creatures. You gave us a home, you gave us your name and most importantly you gave us unqualified love. Whatever we are or have we owe to you,

Dad and the rest of this community. When you arrive in Huron you will find a new home built and furnished to your specifications. This applies to Uncle Chris, Uncle Brad and Aunt Melinda as well." Martha passed the microphone to George who addressed his comments to Chris. "Uncle Chris our company has done so well we want to do this as a way of saying thank you for the life you and the others have made possible for us. We have two crews finishing jobs in Sioux City and Sioux Falls. We can start moving men and equipment to Huron by early March. All we need from you and the other are the specifications and location of the houses and the square footage required for the plant. If we are unable to find a building to rehab we will erect a new one. I will sit down with the women and sketch their wishes with respect to the houses. Our engineers will take care of the plant."

Chris felt it was necessary to explain his plans to the group. He told them if he was fortunate to live that long he expected to live in Huron for only four or possibly five years. At that time he would turn complete control of the operation over to Dallon and return to his home in Wolf Song. It had been his home for the better part of sixty years and it was where he wanted to end his days. It seemed extravagant to him to build three houses for that short span of time but he would defer to the judgment of the young people on the matter.

The shelter house was buzzing with talk. There were tears at the prospect of losing grandparents and parents for four or five years. Dallon pointed out that it was only a two hour flight from Perry to Huron and he was sure the new houses would be built with several spare bedrooms each.

Brendon and Chris agreed to meet the next morning so they could discuss the move. George scheduled a meeting with Phoebe and Melinda to begin sketching the homes to be built for them.

As the people in the shelter house were cleaning up in preparation for returning home they were give a special treat. The seldom heard but still familiar wolf song began. Everyone stopped and sat down to listen to the primitive serenade. Every time Chris listened to the wolves he had to wonder if it would be the last time. There was still a sizable population of wolves in Iowa but now they stayed in the wilder areas in the timber along the rivers.

Eventually the wolf song ended and people departed for their homes. Craig, Janis and their three children were spending the night with Chris so they had only a short walk along the edge of the timber. When they reached the house the three teenagers asked for and were given permission to watch some of the "Three Stooges" videos Chris had in his collection. The adults bundled up, got coffee and went out to sit on the deck. They talked of the past, of their memories of Carol and what changes the future might bring. Janis confided that at forty-three she was pregnant. She told Chris that if the child was a girl she wanted, with his permission, to name the baby Carol Janine after her grandmother. Chris was too filled with emotion to speak but nodded his head yes then got out of his chair to give Janis a hug and a kiss on the cheek. Shortly after that it began to snow. It came down in soft feathery flakes and with no wind the flakes lay where they fell. They soon went inside but left the outside lights burning so they could watch the snow.

Chapter 17 2160

T he next morning there was a six inch blanket of snow covering everything. The air had been so calm there were cones of
snow on top of fence posts.

After breakfast the youngsters went out to clear the deck.
They went to the machine shop for the snow blower and by the
end of the morning had cleared all of the foot paths to every
outbuilding.

As the three of them were having their mid-morning coffee and watching the birds flocking to the feeders Chris posed a
question to the younger two. He asked what they were going to
for space when the baby arrived. Their house in Dallas Center
was already crowded and was situated where expanding it was
impractical. They told him they had been considering building a
house on the western edge of New Home. Chris countered that
idea by proposing they move into his house. When he returned
from South Dakota he could have a small home built along the
edge of the woods and none of them would ever have to move
again. What they finally agreed upon was to add three rooms to
the west side of the existing house. There would be a bedroom,
bath and study for Chris plus another bedroom. Chris would
take his meals with the family and they would all have some degree of privacy.

When the young people came in for lunch they were told of
the impending changes. The first question they asked was who
was to get which room. Elizabeth, or Betsy as she was called, was
only eleven but she was given first choice. The room she chose
was the smallest of the three. It did have a tiny but adequate private bathroom. Jayden, next in age at twelve, took the largest of

the rooms. He said he wanted the extra space to store his collection of antique books. Mark didn't have a choice to make. He was pleased however as the window in his room looked out across the deck with a good view of his grandfather's bird feeders. He asked for and was given the task of keeping the feeders filled and in good repair.

Chapter 18 2160

By the middle of March events were moving at a hectic pace. George and Martha had crews in Huron who were restoring two dormitories and a cafeteria to usable condition. These were located on the campus of the defunct Huron University. Already there was talk of opening the University again if the population increased enough to warrant doing so.

Chris had contacted Lance and convinced him to come out of retirement long enough to get the new plant built and operating. Dallon had flown Chris, Brendon and Lance to Huron. Almost immediately they had found a suitable building for the plant. It was large enough to provide room for expansion in the future. George had crews ready to start working to restore the building to weatherproof condition, then to prepare the inside for the installation of machinery.

With the preliminary work on the plant proceeding the men turned their attention to the task of finding a site for the homes which were to be erected. They drove through the mostly derelict city without finding a spot which suited them. They resorted to driving the country roads and about five miles to the north and east of town they found a promising location on a gently sloping hillside facing east toward the James River. A smaller stream came from the east and emptied into the James. There were approximately sixty acres covered in prairie grass with a few scattered trees. A paved but badly deteriorated road fronted the property at the crest of the hill. About halfway down the hill were two ancient Cottonwood trees spaced two hundred yards or so apart. Chris commented that he would like his house situated so he had a view of the James and the mouth of the little stream which emptied into it framed by the Cottonwoods.

George explained that he planned to build the houses two hundred feet apart with a paved walk connecting the three homes. This would insure some privacy while allowing the older people to walk between the homes. He also felt the homes of the two women should be next to each other with Brad and Melinda's home in the center of the three.

The first order of business would be to drill a well to insure and adequate water supply. At the same time a solar array would be constructed for their power supply. George had men and equipment standing ready in Huron to begin those projects.

Chris planned to file a claim for eighty acres. This was to insure they would not be engulfed by a housing development and provide Brendon with enough land to start a twenty cow breeding herd of Angus cattle.

Chapter 19 2160

By the end of June the three houses were nearing completion and work on the composite plant was progressing rapidly. There had been a steady stream of trucks carrying machines, parts and the soy beans, corn and wood chips needed for producing the composite. A rail line from Mitchell to Huron was being restored to a usable condition and was slated to start operating in August.

At the site of the new homes a deep well had been bored and was producing clean, potable water in a quantity sufficient to supply many times the number of expected consumers. The solar array was in place and operating. The projected move-in day was the first of August. Landscaping around the homes was incomplete but that would be done to suit the residents once they had moved in.

Lance had been looking at a long abandoned set of buildings only a half mile from the entrance to the property of Chris and the others. He had about decided to raze the old house and build a new one on the still solid foundation. On learning of this Chris invited him to build next to the three homes nearing completion in "Wolf Song North" as they had started referring to their new community. Lance's wife Rebecca has insisted they accept the invitation. They had been living in a dormitory filled with young men and women of the construction crews and she was starved for conversation with women closer to her own age of sixty-one.

Chapter 20 2160

As the hectic pace continued in Huron life went on as usual in New Home. In July Lori was admitted to the hospital and delivered identical twin girls. Going to the family archives she went back six generations and named the girls Lori Ann and Betty Kay. By the time they were two weeks old Billie commented that they were going to be great talkers when they reached the age of speech. Neither of them was often quiet. They even tried to gurgle and coo while they were nursing.

Dallon had flown Phoebe and Melinda to Huron twice so they could see the progress on their new homes. On the second visit both women were amazed to see that George had arranged the kitchens to be a complete match for those they had been using in Wolf Song. Both women were in tears and George was showered with hugs and kisses. George was quick to point out that it had been Martha's idea. She felt it would make the move a little less traumatic for the older women.

Brad was eighty years old. He had been a medical doctor for almost sixty of those years and was not yet ready to hang up his stethoscope. He had scoured Huron and on the north side of town had found a former clinic with the rooms still intact. He had prevailed on George to send a crew to clean out and paint the interior. Furniture and medical equipment which was beyond reclamation was discarded and he began a list of what was needed to open a medical clinic.

Brad had made several flights back to New Home on what he called shopping excursions. On one of these trips he had sat down with Kathie, Pearl and their doctor husbands. With surprisingly little effort on his part he had sold them on the idea of moving to Huron and operating the soon to open clinic. Kathie was delighted at the prospect of having her five favorite patients returned to her care and Pearl simply was elated at the prospect of maintaining close contact with her parents.

Chapter 21 2160

On a day in early August the Sweets, Hintz's and Chris were officially moving into their new homes. The movers had departed and although there was yet much to be done they were taking a break and having a coffee on the Weddle deck. They had been joined by Lance. He had driven out to check on the progress of his own house being built next door.

The conversation had shifted to a discussion of the Wolf Song suppers in New Home. They all agreed it had been a wonderful way to see the children and grandchildren on a regular basis. Phoebe and Melinda insisted they need to start a South Dakota version of the supper as soon as possible.

Kathie and Pearl had made it known they wanted homes built close to their parents. Each of the daughters had three children who were teenagers so there would be a good sized group from the beginning. It was agreed on the spot that they must erect a shelter house similar to the one in the Wolf Song community. Before returning to the tasks of getting things arranged in the new homes they agreed to hold the first community supper on Thursday of the second week in October. It would be held at the home of Brad and Melinda.

Progress at the composite plant had proceeded more rapidly than had been anticipated. Lance announced that they would be making a test run during the first week in October and if it went well they should begin full production by November.

The property on which Chris had filed was bordered on the north by a paved county road. The property extended a quarter of a mile south of the road and reached a half mile east. The eastern limit lay across the James River and encompassed the mouth of the smaller stream which came in from the east. Brendon filed on the eighty acres adjacent to the Weddle property on the north and Brad did the same to the south. All of the properties were enclosed by new fences except along the river. Cross fences were installed about fifty yards from the west property line with several gates to allow access between the properties.

Kathie, Pearl and their families were in Huron on the day of the first community supper. They were there to check on the final preparations of the clinic prior to opening. They were also searching for temporary housing. Several tutors had been retained to continue the education of Pearl and Kathie's teenagers. The ten visitors were staying at the homes of the elders. Brendon Jr. had sent a supply of fresh and smoked meats plus several dozen eggs to be shared by his parents, Chris, Brad and Melinda.

It was a cool, crisp afternoon and sixteen people were gathered on the deck of the Sweet home visiting and drinking coffee or tea.

Kathie's thirteen year old daughter Persephone had been sitting by herself while watching the myriad of waterfowl which were moving up and down the river. She broke into the group conversation to announce that there were animals of some sort moving through the trees on the far side of the river. Brad picked up the binoculars which were kept on the deck for just this sort of event. After looking for a few moments he revealed that the animals were Bison. Everyone rushed to the deck railing to look. As they stood watching, the animals walked out of the trees to the edge of the river and stopped to drink. After drinking, the little herd, the people had counted thirteen animals, plunged into the river and swam across. After crossing the stream the herd made its way through the trees and out into the open where the animals began to graze.

By the time the group had finished supper and were sitting on the deck with coffee, dusk was settling in.

The little Bison herd had moved almost halfway between the river and the house. Now, most of them were lying down while lazily chewing their cud.

There was a nip in the air and everyone was bundled up against the chill. It had been a pleasant afternoon and evening and no one was yet ready to call it a day. Phoebe told Persephone that since she had been the first to spot the buffalo it had earned her the right to name the supper. Persephone asked if she could have some time to consider a name and thanked Phoebe for the privilege of doing so.

As they were picking up the coffee things and dessert plates Melinda commented that it had been an almost perfect day. She had been surrounded by family, old and dear friends plus perfect weather. Phoebe interjected at that point to say they were only missing one thing. As if on cue a familiar sound filled the air. It was the cry of a wolf pack in full song. Everyone stopped where they were and most sat down. After a half hour it was over. Phoebe had tears on her cheeks and Chris had a lump in his throat. Persephone was the first to speak. She said, "Buffalo Song, I know bison don't sing but I believe that song was for them." Everyone agreed and the new family supper had a name.

Chapter 22 2161

|n January the weather, which had been bitter cold in November and December, relented. The snow which had accumulated in the cold months melted away and it seemed more like late March than the middle of winter.

The composite plant was now operating two ten hour shifts six days per week. They were unable to keep up with demand. Contractors were doing very little construction but they were all trying to stockpile material in preparation for spring.

All that was being produced were sheets and smaller members which were suitable for framing. George and his crews were rushing to prepare another building where larger structural timbers would be produced.

The little bison herd had remained through the winter. With the gates in the line fences opened, the animals had access to all of the property claimed by the group. There were two underpasses built into the road on the north side of the plot claimed by Chris which provided over two hundred acres of grass for the herd.

Brendon decided he would rather watch buffalo than Angus cattle so the idea of a beef herd was soon forgotten. Brendon went so far as to purchase hay and a small amount of corn to supplement the grass diet of the animals. It had soon become apparent that the leader of the herd was an old cow with crooked horns. Instead of the graceful inward curving horns common to the animal this cow had horns which curved upward for five or six inches then turned sharply forward for about a foot. It was soon noticed that she was not reluctant to use those twin spikes to move the other herd members in the direction she wanted them to go. She was soon given the name "Old Crook" and she was the unchallenged queen of her part of the prairie.

With the coming of spring corn and soy beans were the predominant crops being planted. There had been an influx of people planning to farm before there was adequate housing for them. Temporary housing was erected to shelter people while their homes were being built. Out houses, recalling the eighteen and nineteen hundreds were erected and people lived as crudely as the country folks from two and three hundred years in the past.

Eventually crops were planted, homes were completed and life returned to normal. There were many people who in later years would recall the dark days of 2161.

Chapter 23 2165

Chris and the others had now been in South Dakota for almost five years. At the January Buffalo Song supper Chris spoke to the group. He told them he had been considering his original plan to stay five years then return to Iowa. He had given the idea much thought and had come to the conclusion that he wanted to stay in his present home. It did not hold the memories of the house in Wolf Song but in many ways it was easier to cope with the fact of Carol's absence.

When Chris finished speaking there was utter silence in the shelter house. Even the children were quiet as if they sensed that something momentous was occurring.

It was Melinda who broke the silence. She rose from her seat and walked over to Chris, took his hand in hers and kissed him on the cheek. She thanked him for bringing her home to the South Dakota prairie. She told Chris they had traveled many miles together and she didn't regret a single one. Now she was within one hundred fifty miles of where she had been born and didn't ever want to leave again. As Melinda took her seat Phoebe stood. Before Phoebe could speak Brendon was on his feet and said, "Let me do this." Phoebe nodded and sat down while taking Brendon's hand and holding it. With no preamble Brendon began, "Only my doctors and Phoebe are aware of this. I have been diagnosed with early dementia. At times I see faces I should recognize and do not remember them. I sit out on the deck and look out over the land and the river. I then turn to Phoebe and ask what became of the basalt cliffs along the river and when did the Columbia become so small. It is only going to get worse as time passes. My doctors' feel that moving back to Iowa would only add to the confusion so Phoebe and I have decided to remain here whatever the rest of you choose to do."

As Brendon took his seat Billie and Lori Brown came to stand behind him. Lori, with her had on Brendon's shoulder spoke to the group and to Brendon. "Uncle Brendon, I have been a member of this group for the least amount of time of anyone from my generation, however I think I speak for all of us. You are loved and respected by every one of us. What you have done for us and for this new country cannot be measured and can never be paid back. We will be here for you and with you the rest of your life."

The group sat quietly except for muted sobbing from a few of them. Again, as if on cue, the Wolf Song began. When it was over the people gathered their belongings and made their ways home.

Chapter 24 2165

While the people of New Home had fixed their eyes on the west and northwest others had looked to the east. With no one to cut them the pine and hardwood forests had made remarkable recoveries. Likewise, after fifty plus years of no appreciable fishing the great populations of cod and other fish species had recovered to levels not seen in over three hundred years.

There was a steady movement of people to the east and northeast. Most of these were immigrants from coastal areas of South Africa, Zimbabwe and South America. New states were formed with new names. New Jersey, Delaware and Maryland combined to form a new entity named the Mid-Atlantic Commonwealth. Massachusetts, Rhode Island and Connecticut became simply New England while Vermont and New Hampshire united to form Upper New England.

Thanks to the burgeoning air freight industry the states in the middle of the country had access to moderately priced seafood both fresh and frozen.

Billie and Lori announced they were going to open a new company terminal when the airport being built was completed. This facility was located just north of the now deserted village of Virgil. When the population growth made it feasible they wanted to open a final terminal in Billings, Montana.

Chapter 25 2165

In the year 2105 two events occurred which would have a profound effect on the people of Buffalo Song some sixty years later.

In the province of Manitoba two female wolves were in their dens giving birth. The wolves were half-sisters and their dens were located some five miles apart. The dens were located near the shore of Lake Winnipeg on the peninsula separating Lake Winnipeg from the string of lakes to the west.

The only thing unique to the two litters was that in each litter there were two female pups which were abnormally large. They were half again as large as their siblings. Their size might have made them a prime target for human hunters but when the animals were a year old humans virtually disappeared from the planet. When these large specimens began breeding at age two their offspring made another significant jump in size. This continued through six or seven generations until the animal was truly a monstrous beast. It stood three and a half feet tall at the shoulder and weighed an average of three hundred-fifty pounds. It ate everything from mice to bison and moose. The favored prey were wild cattle which were slow and easy to bring down.

It seemed the giant canines were destined to become the dominant life force in North America. They were held back by two circumstances. First was that they produced very small litters, bearing only two and occasionally three pups at a time. The second was a short life span, they seldom lived beyond six or seven years. There were seldom more than one hundred-fifty animals at any given time and from time to time rabies would devastate the packs. From their original location in Manitoba their range gradually moved south and brought them into conflict with humans who were now moving back onto the prairie.

Chapter 26 2166

In early spring stories began to circulate in the Huron area of the presence to the north of a giant wolf. For the most part the stories were relegated to the status of those about the Sasquatch of the northwest. No one seemed to have actually seen the animal and there was no physical evidence or photographs of the beast. It had become a common topic of conversation although seldom a serious one.

It was a warm morning in late June. Linda Ann had visited that morning. In reality, she, like his other children and grandchildren had really stopped in to check on Chris. She had insisted on making him breakfast and had sat with him as he ate. She confided that she was bored with life and the practice of law in Iowa. She was considering opening an office in Huron but first she had to find suitable housing. Chris was quick to point out that he had a suite of rooms going unused and she was welcome to move in and stay for as long as she wished. She had quickly accepted the offer and then left to return to Iowa and begin closing down her practice there.

Chris enjoyed spending the late morning hours sitting on the shaded portion of the deck. From that viewpoint he could look out over the pasture and the river. He usually managed to have a good nap during this time. The first thing he always did after sitting was to look for the little Bison herd. The herd, now numbering some twenty-five animals, had adopted the three adjoining properties as home and displayed no inclination to move on. Chris was of the opinion that the hay and grain put out by Brendon on a regular basis was a major factor in keeping the animals from wondering away.

The first thing Chris noticed on this day was that the herd was milling about in the corner of the fence between his property and Brad's. Two of the older bulls and three of the cows in the outer edge of the herd were facing out with their heads down as if in a defensive position. Down the hill at a distance of some seventy-five yards stood a lone cow. Her stance looked awkward and she seemed to stagger when she tried to move. Chris picked up the binoculars to get a closer look. He could also see what looked like blood on the animal's flanks and hindquarters. He could also see what looked like an animal of some sort on the ground beyond the cow. The cow finally moved enough that he could see the horns and identify her as Old Crook. Chris could also see the other animal was a wolf but unlike any he had ever seen. The animal was a giant. It appeared to be almost half the size of the buffalo cow. There also appeared to be blood on the shoulder and side of the wolf.

As Chris was observing the bison and wolf he became aware of the sound of a moving vehicle. Looking around he saw Brendon in his little electric ATV heading across the pasture and down the hill toward where the bison cow was standing. Chris stood and shouted but there was no response from Brendon. Chris hurried into the house and grabbed a rifle out of the gun cabinet. It was the old Marlin he had carried so many miles in the dark years fol-lowing 2106. He always kept it cleaned and loaded for emergen-cies. Grabbing a chair pillow to use as a barrel rest Chris rushed outside and took his seat at the table.

Brendon was continuing down the hill and it was obvious to Chris that Brendon did not see the wolf crouching on the far side of the buffalo. As Brendon came close the buffalo took two or three tottering steps and collapsed, this finally exposed the wolf to Brendon's view. He reacted by wrenching the steering wheel hard to the right which was uphill. He had unstrapped his safety belt as he prepared to stop. As the vehicle turned uphill the right front wheel ran into a large rock which flipped the ATV over onto the driver's side. Brendon was thrown half out of his seat and when the vehicle landed the side rail of the roll cage hit Brendon squarely across the neck.

Brendon died almost instantly as the ATV rolled clear of his body. As this was happening Chris finally had a clear view of the wolf and fired one shot which hit the animal in the center of the chest. The beast took two or three faltering steps and collapsed.

Chris sat and stared, stunned by what he had just witnessed. He became aware of movement in the trees along the river and suddenly two more of the great predators appeared and began trotting up the hill toward the scene of death. Knowing that he was not a marksman on moving targets Chris waited. When the wolves arrived at the death scene they sniffed the dead wolf and ignoring the now dead buffalo walked over to Brendon's body and began to examine it. When one of them appeared as if it was going to take a bite Chris fired again. With its head down the bullet took the animal in the brain and it died where it stood. The second animal turned in a circle several times as if searching for this new threat. When it stopped the wolf was broadside to Chris who promptly put a round through the animal's rib cage. The animal started to race away but after no more than twenty-five feet it piled into a heap.

Again Chris sat for a few minutes as if in a stupor, trying to comprehend what had just happened. Chris finally stirred from his seat. His first move was to get more ammunition and reload the Marlin. He wanted to check Brendon's body before informing Phoebe about what had happened. He was actually surprised that he had not heard from her about the rifle shots as their house was only a few hundred feet from his own. As he was about to go through the gate to the pasture Melinda appeared on the back sidewalk. She indeed was curious about the shots and had been unable to come out sooner. She had been helping Brad into the hydro-therapy tub which he used every day for relief to his amputated leg and formerly crippled hip.

Chris quickly related a summary of the events of the morning and told Melinda he needed to go check on Brendon's body before Phoebe appeared. Melinda told him there was no hurry as Phoebe's three grandsons were in town and Phoebe had gone to have lunch with them. She also advised him to drive his own

ATV down to the death scene. It would offer him more protection and faster escape if needed.

As Chris was backing his four seat ATV out of the garage Lance appeared in the rear view mirror. Chris quickly explained what had happened and where he was going. Lance told Chris if would wait while he went to fetch a weapon he would go with him. Lance was accompanied by his two daughters. Both women were trauma nurses in the emergency room. They had planned to hike for a couple of miles along the river and were dressed appropriately. The women looked so much alike that Chris could never remember which of them was Jayme and which was Holly. Lance soon returned and they set off down the hill.

Chapter 27 2166

On arriving at the scene the two nurses checked Brendon and confirmed that he was dead. They agreed that he had probably died instantly from a broken neck and a partially crushed skull.

Brendon's body was lifted and placed in the bed of the ATV. Even with the tailgate lowered his feet and ankles extended over the end. It had now been an hour since the accident. Chris said, "We need to get him home, Phoebe doesn't need to see him like this. We will take him to my house."

They carried the body into a spare bedroom and after stripping the bed place the body on it. Jayme told Chris if he would bring a pan plus some towels and wash cloths she and Holly would bathe Brendon before Phoebe saw him. When the nurses had finished they put clean underwear, given to them by Chris, on the body and covered all but the head with a light blanket.

They had no more than finished tidying up the room when Phoebe appeared at the front door. Her first words to Chris were, "What happened to Brendon, is he dead?" Chris was stunned and could only shake his head yes.

Chris led Phoebe to the room where Brendon lay. She gasped when she first looked at the body then asked if she could be alone with Brendon for a while. Chris moved a chair over beside the bed then left, closing the door behind him.

Chris explained to the three young men what had occurred. While they drove the ATV down to the spot where their grandfather had died Chris and Lance discussed what their next step should be. The community had to be warned, and soon. They decided the marshal's office would be the place to start.

The local marshal was a man named Jacob Howard. Chris had met him back in the days when the Marshal Service was being formed to combat the bandit gangs in the west. Chris briefly explained and Jake told him he would be on the way within minutes. True to his word, in less than twenty minutes the Marshal's personal helicopter was landing in the pasture behind the houses. This disturbed the bison herd enough that they galloped down the hill and began to mill about in the area along the river.

Jake had brought a photographer with him who was soon busy taking pictures and making measurements of the dead wolves. Jake said his first step would be to send pictures and text to the Federal government in Lexington and alert them to the situation. His next move would be to pre-empt time from every television and radio station west of Minnesota and Iowa. He would broadcast pictures and text concerning the wolves and advise that no one leave the shelter of buildings unless they were armed.

When Jake left to begin sounding the alarm Lance and Chris returned to the house.

Chapter 28 2166

Lance told Chris he was going home for a while and would come back later to offer his condolences to Phoebe. When Chris entered the house he found the living room overflowing. In addition to the six people he had expected to find Chris was greeted by Brad and Melinda, both of his sons and their families plus Billie and Lori Brown and their three children. The group filled the living room dining area plus the stools at the breakfast bar.

The television was turned on to the local station which was running the story of the wolves. Jake was shown making a statement which amounted to a warning that no should venture out unless adequately armed and children should be permitted outside only with an armed guard present. All schools and public gatherings were closed until further notice. The program only ran for twenty minutes and was then repeated over and over. The national news ran the same information and pictures. The only additional information was that the government was organizing a group of hunters which would be sent to South Dakota to confront the menace.

Phoebe brought the group's focus back to Brendon by telling Chris she would like to have Brendon's body moved to her house. She wanted him to spend his last night with them in his own bed. This was accomplished by the three grandsons using an improvised stretcher. Phoebe dressed Brendon in his favorite shirt and jeans then invited anyone who wished to do so to sit with him. The only problem to arise was that Cody Lee who was now ten could not understand why his gramps would not wake up. Cody had been Brendon's favorite great-grandchild and much attention had been lavished on him. Cody finally curled up in Brendon's big chair and holding a wooden duck which Brendon had carved for him, went to sleep.

The afternoon passed and as dusk approached people began leaving. Those who were driving wanted to be home before dark. Those who lived in the six house neighborhood were escorted home by heavily armed men. Jayme and Holly were the last to leave. They were accompanied by young Brendon and Jonathon whose mother, Mavis, took notice that the men didn't return to Phoebe's house until well after two a.m. Mavis paced and fretted until Phoebe told her to relax and that there had been sparks flying between the four young people all afternoon and evening.

Dallon and Linda Ann went home with Chris. They put on a pot of coffee then sat discussing the day's events. Chris was still in shock over Brendon's death. They had lived next door to each other and been at least as close as brothers for fifty-two years. Chris turned on all of the outside lights which illuminated all of the yard and part way down the hill. As they sat looking out they became aware of activity in the area where the dead animals lay. They could not make out details but caught frequent reflections of eyes when the animals looked toward the house.

Chapter 29 2166

It had been a late night so there were few early risers the next morning. At around nine Chris was just sitting down to his first cup of coffee when he heard two rifle shots. Picking up the Marlin he stepped out onto the deck to see Phoebe hurrying along the back walk toward his house. She was carrying the little rifle Brendon had picked up for her those many years ago in Oregon. Chris walked out to meet her, thinking she might be frightened or upset. Instead, he was met by the same unflappable Phoebe he had always known. When he asked her what had happened. She told him she had opened the door for some fresh air and could hear the wolves growling. She had picked up her rifle and stepped out to the deck where she could see the beasts squabbling over the carcass of the buffalo cow. She sat down at a table and saw the two of the animals had spotted her movement and were looking up the hill directly at her. She quickly aimed and shot one of them in the head. At the sound of the shot all of the animals directed their gaze up the hill and stood without moving. She aimed at a second wolf and pulled the trigger. At the sound of the second shot the rest of the pack, eight animals in all, had turned and fled down the hill toward the river. Phoebe was sure both shots had been fatal but she did not want to go by herself to find out. Chris suggested that he and Phoebe were old enough to sit on the deck with coffee while her grandsons went to check on the wolves. The men reported that indeed there were five dead wolves at the scene. They used the ATV and dragged the carcass of the buffalo down to the edge of the brush along the river. This would allow the vultures and coyotes to pick the bones clean without becoming a nuisance up near the houses.

Chris received a call from Jake Howard that he would be out with three government hunters in early afternoon. These were professional hunters who were kept on retainer by the Interior Department to deal with problem bears and big cats. When Jake arrived with the three hunters they were taken to where the animals were lying. The men were stunned by the actual size of the beasts. They had seen the pictures transmitted the day before but the pictures simply did not offer a true perspective of the size of the wolves. The bodies were loaded on a trailer to be taken to the airport from where they would be flown to a facility for studies including DNA testing to try and determine their origins. Patrick, who as the senior member of the hunter group was also the supervisor, surmised that the bodies now gave some credence to the stories which had filtered down from the north. It probably also explained the tales of missing hikers and fishermen. They agreed that the animals probably hid out and slept during the day and did their hunting at night.

Because of the large area they would have to cover and the scarcity of roads in the region it was decided to ask for helicopters to use in the search. The Interior Department maintained a fleet of twenty small helicopters which were used for many purposes. Ten of these were immediately dispatched to Huron for the wolf hunt. There were also six of the Night Owl choppers assigned to the task. The early versions of this bird had been fitted with a pod holding two twenty mm guns. These had been replaced by a pair of fifty caliber weapons which allowed for more rounds of ammunition to be carried.

The search was carried out in a grid pattern with two helicopters flying in tandem over each area assigned to them.

The two assets, speed and endurance, which enabled the wolves to be successful hunters would, in the end, lead to their destruction. They could outrun any animal on the plains except Antelope. With Antelope they would run the animals to the point of exhaustion then move in for the kill.

Chapter 30 2166

Six days after the hunt began the hunters had their first success. Some twenty miles south of Huron a pair of the hunter birds accompanied by two Night Owls flushed the eight wolves which had been involved in killing the buffalo. The hunters were flying in line with a separation of a half mile at a very low altitude. The first helicopter had just passed a wild plum thicket which had grown up in a fence line. As the second chopper approached the wolves panicked, broke cover and began to run.

Having no real fear of anything the wolves ran at a leisurely lope which they could maintain for hours.

Flying just high enough to clear the poles of a long dead power line, the first Night Owl lined up behind the fleeing wolves. Using his optical sight the gunner walked a stream of fifty caliber fire from the back to the front of the pack. There was no need for a firing run by the second Night Owl, every one of the wolves was on the ground, dead or dying.

The helicopters landed and the animals examined. Two of the creatures were still weakly thrashing about. Each of them was dispatched by a single pistol shot. A call was placed to their headquarters in Huron and trucks were sent to pick up the animal carcasses for testing.

Two days later twenty and forty miles to the west two more wolf packs were flushed into the open. These were larger groups with sixteen animals in one pack and eighteen in the other. The end results were the same with all of the animals being killed. DNA samples were taken but the bodies were taken by local people who wanted to tan the hides and display the skulls with their long, lethal looking fangs.

The search continued for weeks with no additional animals being found. In the search some ten thousand square miles were thoroughly searched and most of the eastern half of the state was given a cursory inspection.

What the humans could not know was that in a period of two weeks they had wiped out the total population of the species which had only existed for some sixty years. Forty-seven animals seemed so few that for years stories would arise of sightings which were all fictitious or imagined.

One fact remained. The gene pool which had created the monster wolf was still alive and functioning up in Manitoba. There was always a chance the beast could return.

Chapter 31 2166

It was now the middle of May. A month had passed since the episode with the wolves. People still went armed when they went out away from the houses but tension had eased considerably after the wolf packs had been seen and eliminated thirty miles to the south.

Chris had dug out the old Colt .22 pistol he had carried many years in the past. He didn't feel it was really necessary but it gave him a sense of comfort to feel the weight of it on his hip.

One tragic event marred the otherwise uneventful appearance of the wolves. A young farmer whose wife had been terrified by the report of the animals decided to show her there was nothing of which to be afraid. One evening at dusk while holding a dark piece of canvas over his head and shoulders he stood behind the corner of a chicken house. On hearing her approach he had jumped out while making a loud woofing noise. He was greeted by the blast from both barrels of a twenty gauge shotgun and died instantly. The official inquest ruled that he was killed in an accident. Public opinion deemed that he had died from stupidity.

Phoebe was faced with the decision of where to place Brendon's cremated remains. There was a niche reserved for both of them in the Memorial at Wolf Song but she was no longer certain that was the place for them. She invited Melinda, Brad and Chris over for coffee and pie and while they were eating brought up the subject. Melinda immediately stated that she and Brad had no intention of ever again leaving their beloved South Dakota prairie. Chris was of a like mind and had no wish to be placed anywhere else.

George was called in and agreed to construct a small memorial wall to contain the urns. He had already suspected that this situation might arise and had prepared sketches of what he had in mind. The sketches were approved and work began immediately. George planned to use granite from a quarry in the Black Hills where he already had a crew working. He also was going to put in a small grove of Aspen trees and pipe water from the community well to keep them healthy in dry times.

For a location they chose the spot where the buffalo cow had died fighting the wolves. A five acre plot was fenced and work began soon after.

When Billie Brown heard what was being done he went to Chris and asked if he could be allowed to move the ashes of his parents to this new memorial ground. Billie felt it would please Pete and Jackie to rest with the three couples with whom they had traveled so far and seen so many changes. Chris replied that on his list of things to do was a note to ask Billie if he wanted to do this very thing.

Chapter 32 2168

For the first year after the death of Brendon, Cody had been lost in his own world. He had finally been made to realize that Brendon was gone and was never coming back. His parents and the other adults were not sure whether Cody had actually grasped the concept of death or if he thought Gramps had gone somewhere and would not be returning. Chris had driven him down to the memorial and shown him the urn containing Brendon's ashes. Cody had shaken his head no and very firmly stated, "Not big enough for Gramps."

The two of them spent many hours together. Whenever Christopher and Carolyn visited Phoebe, Cody soon escaped and found his way to Chris's house. Linda Ann, who had never married, was living permanently with her father. She decorated one of the bedrooms for the boy and even included a photograph of his beloved Gramps. Clothing was gathered so the boy could change if he got dirty or tore a knee in his pants. He often spent the night even though his parents were staying only two houses away.

The old man and the boy spent countless hours on the deck watching the birds at the feeders. Chris showed Cody that if he sat very still with seeds in his hand the Chickadees would eat from his hand. The first time this happened Cody insisted on leaving immediately so he could tell his mom and Grams.

Cody also discovered the video library and soon became addicted to the movies of The Three Stooges. He watched them so many times that he would utter lines of dialogue before the actors said them. He would also shout "look out" when he knew a slap or a pie was forthcoming.

In mid-April of 2168 the little Buffalo herd disappeared. One day they were grazing in the area below the two large cottonwood trees and the next they were nowhere to be found. Chris drove over all three properties and could find no trace of the animals. There were no downed fences or broken gates. A week later Carolyn and Christopher were visiting Phoebe when the subject of the missing herd was brought up. Christopher offered to investigate. He drove down to the river then began searching the woods on foot. He soon discovered where the animals had forded the river then turned north. Dallon was called and he agreed to fly Chris on an aerial search for the herd. They flew directly north from Huron and some seventy or eighty miles from home they spotted the herd plodding stolidly along. Chris could identify some of the animals and thus knew he had found the correct herd. They returned home and Chris found it difficult to look out over the prairie and not see the great shaggy beasts.

One benefit of the animals being gone was that Chris had no fear of Cody being out in the pastures alone. Chris purchased a two seat ATV then had the transmission altered so the machine would only operate in low and reverse gears which allowed a speed of about that of a person walking.

Chris gave Cody extensive driving lessons. It was also stressed that when he heard the old fashioned farm bell ring he must return to the house immediately.

On the day of Cody's first solo trip Chris was standing beside the machine imparting last minute instructions. Cody reached out took his hand and said, "You are my New Gramps now and I love you." With that the boy drove away and left his New Gramps standing with a lump in his throat and tears in the corners of his eyes.

Linda Ann saw her father standing at the gate for a long time and walked out to check on him. She took one look at his face and said, "Daddy what is wrong?" Chris replied, "Not a thing baby girl, not a thing. Why don't we go have some coffee and one of those sweet rolls Phoebe brought over this morning?"

Chapter 33 2168

The machine opened an entirely new world for the boy. It was slow and quiet and thus did not disturb the wildlife as did the larger, faster ATVs.

Cody saw any number of creatures he had never noticed before. There were small lizards scampering about in the grass along the edge of the woods beside the river. There were two different kinds of ground squirrels plus a meadow lark which sang every day from the same post. His most favorite animals to watch were the prairie dogs whose little colony occupied one lower corner of Brad and Melinda's property.

It was here in the dog town where Cody created the first intimate contact with the wild creatures of his domain.

He parked the ATV and walked into the middle of the colony. On a large mound he stopped and looked into a hole where a prairie dog had just disappeared. He could see or hear nothing but he sat down and waited. After perhaps five minutes the furry head appeared again. On seeing Cody still there the animal again went down the hole. This was repeated four or five times until Cody had a bright idea. He had two of Phoebe's peanut butter cookies in his shirt pocket and everyone loved Gram's cookies. He broke off a piece of a cookie and placed it in the mouth of the hole. Sure enough when the prairie dog appeared again it smelled the cookie and began eating it. When Cody moved the dog was gone in a flash. They repeated this routine a number of times with Cody placing the cookie farther out of the hole each time. Finally the animal stayed where it was as Cody tossed more cookie in front of it.

After two days the prairie dog, obviously a nursing mother, would take bits of cookie from his fingers and sit close to him as she ate them. Cody was beside himself with joy. Ten days later she was followed out of the den by three miniature versions of herself. The little ones displayed no fear of the boy and were soon scrambling in his lap for bits of cookie.

One morning Phoebe wrapped two cookies and as she moved to put them in his pocket Cody grasped her hand and said, "not enough, need more, need two more." Phoebe was puzzled but placed four cookies in his pocket. She was thanked by a big smile, a big kiss and "I love you Grams," from Cody.

Later that morning Phoebe walked over to have coffee and catch up on family news with Chris. As they talked she mentioned the cookie incident that morning and wondered if perhaps she was providing the boy too many treats. Chris said he didn't think so but that he wanted her to see something before she decided. Chris brought his spotting scope from the cabinet, placed it in front of Phoebe and told her to focus on the dog town. After watching for several long minutes Phoebe turned to Chris and with tears in her eyes said, "I don't believe it, that boy has made pets of an entire colony of wild prairie dogs." Chris responded that it appeared that way but in his own mind the animals had become friends more so than pets. Phoebe asked how Cody had accomplished this feat. Chris replied, "With great patience and his Gram's peanut butter cookies." Cody had developed the habit of telling Chris in great detail about each new animal, bird or other creature he encountered. His vocabulary was limited and the description of colors was completely beyond his comprehension. One day Chris had what turned out to be one of the greatest ideas of his life. He went to the shop Margaret and Megan had opened in Huron and purchased a sketch pad and a box of drawing pencils. Maggie teasingly asked him if he was going to take up drawing this late in his life. Chris just smiled and left the store with his purchases.

Chris clipped the sketch pad to a piece of composite sheet for a firm support and gave the pad, pencils and a pencil sharpener to Cody who was puzzled as to what to do with them. Chris told him to draw pictures of the things he saw.

Cody's first efforts were frustrating to say the last. He broke far more pencil leads than he wore down. Chris bought more pencils and urged him to keep trying.

One day in October of 2168 Chris looked out one morning and there, to his amazement, was the little buffalo herd. They were milling about the hay and feed bunks as if they were confused about why the bunks were empty. Chris soon had both hay and pellets of commercial feed put out and the animals were lined up eating as if they had never been gone.

Chris realized he was going to need help if he was to continue feeding the animals. His eighty-four year old body simply did not have the strength to manage the heavy bales.

Chapter 39 2169

The winter had been a relatively mild one. In early March Chris noticed the bison herd was restless and edgy. They moved from corner to corner in the three properties and acted cross with each other. They shoved and butted for no apparent reason.

One morning as Brad and Chris were sitting at coffee on the deck they watched as the herd forced a way through the dense riverside brush, crossed the river and turned north. It appeared something had awakened the ancient instinct of the animals to migrate north in the summer and return south in autumn.

Later in the morning Cody appeared and as usual, he was carrying his sketch pad. Chris had numbered the pads as he gave them to the boy. He noted that this was number four. Chris had never seen any of the work in the pads. He felt when Cody was ready to share he would show what he was doing. Cody placed the pad on the table and opened it. Chris was amazed. There in front of him were perfect pencil portraits of a Black Footed Ferret and a Chickadee perched on a human finger. Chris praised the pictures and leafing back through the pad he saw there were pictures of every creature which inhabited Cody's part of the prairie. Each picture showed improvement over those on preceding pages.

Cody accepted the praise with thank you and a beaming smile. After Chris closed the pad he passed it back to Cody and said, "You should be very proud, that is true art." Cody held the pad to his chest and replied, "Could be better, pictures need color." Chris suggested that they show the drawings to Cody's Aunt Maggie. Being an artist herself, she might have some suggestions for Cody.

When she was shown the sketch book Maggie was amazed. She was completely stunned when told that the entire process was self-taught. Maggie commented that if she had the drawings in her gallery they would sell immediately and for good prices. At this point Cody spoke up. He said, "Can't sell, there are for New Gramps, he gave me the pencils and paper and told me to draw."

Maggie went to her supply room and on her return handed Cody a box. When he looked he discovered the box held several dozen pencils. Every color imaginable was included and Maggie simply said, "Make your animals come alive."

That is what Cody proceeded to do. He became the portraitist of the wildlife of South Dakota. In an amazingly short time he grasped the concept of blending two colors to create a third. By late summer Maggie had framed and hung several of his pictures in her gallery. Maggie was soon besieged with requests for prices and the name of the artist. She simply replied that the pictures were not for sale and that for now the artist preferred to remain anonymous.

Unknown to Chris, and the other adults, Cody had been a witness three years ago of the battle between Old Crook and the three giant wolves. He had been watching from a small depression in the hillside when the old cow had made her final stand. He had been afraid to move. After Brendon and Chris had become involved and Chris had shot the three wolves Cody had crept back to Phoebe's house. He had never mentioned the event because he was afraid he would be prohibited from going into the pasture alone.

The scene had remained vivid in his mind and he finally resolved to put it on paper. He obtained a two by thee foot sheet of heavy paper from his Aunt Margaret and taped it to the table in his room. For most of three days he didn't come out of his room except to eat and to tell his mother goodbye. Carolyn told him he could stay at Gram's for the rest of the week.

When Cody was satisfied that the picture was finished he asked Phoebe if he could call New Gramps to come over so he could be the first one to see it.

Chris was led to Cody's room where Cody removed a towel he had placed over the picture. Chris could only gaze in awe at what was before him. The picture showed the Buffalo cow with her spear like horns imbedded in the shoulder and ribs of a giant wolf while two others ripped at her bloodied flanks. After looking for some time Chris finally said, "You were there, you saw this." Cody pointed to a blurred image off to one side, then explained, "There I am, hiding, I was afraid."

Maggie was called to come and see the picture. After gazing at it for some time she began to speak. She said, "This settles it. This boy's work need to be seen and recognized for what it is, a collection of masterpieces. I am going to put on an exhibit featuring only Cody's work. It will be publicized in the newspapers and on television. Everything he has done must be signed. There must be no doubt as to the creator of these works. This latest picture and several others must have titles. Some people are going to say I am the boy's aunt and that I am biased for that reason. That may be correct but my rebuttal is that I recognize true genius when I see it. Now let's get organized, we have a lot of work to do. Cody, you need to learn how to tie a necktie. You are going to be famous and you will need to dress the part."

Maggie planned to hold the exhibit for two weeks with an auction of Cody's work to be held on the final evening of the event. She reasoned that initially the attendance would be small but as more people saw the work the word would spread and the attendance would grow. This was exactly what happened. In the end the auction was moved to a local theater which had been renovated by a local acting group.

Cody had been seated at a table in the gallery and spent his time drawing pictures from memory, drawing both pencil sketches and full color picture. One day as he was busy sketching a hen pheasant sitting on a nest he was interrupted by having a color picture of a Red Fox pushed in front of him. A young female voice asked, "How much is this and will you sign it please?" Before looking up Cody noticed the hand holding the pictures very much resembled his own short plump fingers. As Cody looked up he became aware that he was seeing a person who carried the same genetic combination as himself. He didn't think of it in those terms but he knew that here was another of his kind. Cody stared until the girl blushed and started to turn away. Cody grasped her arm and said, "Don't go, I can't sell the picture until the auction." The girl replied, "That pretty lady over there told me to ask you what it cost."

Cody looked over to see his Aunt Margaret smiling at him and it might be added, looking very pleased with herself. Cody motioned Margaret over and when she arrived she asked if anything was wrong. Cody told Maggie the girl wanted a price for the fox picture and he had told her he could not sell it.

Margaret put her hand on the boy's shoulder and said, "Cody, you need to understand, until these pictures go through the auction they belong to you. You may do anything with them you wish."

At this point the woman with whom Maggie had been chatting joined the group. She congratulated Cody for his wonderful pictures. She told him her name was Adeline Dunworthy and her daughter's name was Kristi. She told them Kristi was so taken by the picture of the fox because she had seen one in their back yard only the week before. Watching the fox trying to catch a large grasshopper had brought the first smile to her face since the death of her father the previous month.

Cody now entered the conversation. He had taken note of Kristi's lush, dark hair, her twinkling blue eyes and her smile, most of all her smile. Cody asked how to spell Kristi's name and Adeline printed it for him on a slip of paper.

Cody placed the fox picture on his table then in the lower corner laboriously printed, Kristi, you are pretty when you smile. He signed it Cody with a flourish and handed it to Kristi.

Adelie commented that they still had to settle on a price. Cody immediately said, "No price, no cost." Adeline responded that he simply couldn't give his work away. Cody pointed at his chest with a stubby finger and replied, "Picture belonged to Cody and Cody says no charge. It now belongs to Kristi. As my Gramps Brendon used to tell me about more cookies, case closed." With that the boy folded his arms across his chest and sat back on his stool as if daring anyone else to argue. No one did.

Adeline and Kristi returned the next day. They had been invited by Maggie to spend that last two days of the exhibit with her. They pulled up another stool and Kristi spent the day sitting with Cody. Cody informed everyone that the picture of the buffalo and wolves would not be sold. His intent was to give it to New Gramps. The picture had been titled Last Stand on the Prairie.

Chris explained to the boy he was giving up a lot of money but Cody was determined that Chris have the picture. Cody explained by simply stating that he and Gramps had shared the scene.

The auction was a complete success and Margaret compiled a long list of requests for more pictures. Cody was going to be busy for some time. Adeline, who operated a hair salon in Mitchell, announced that she would be moving her business to Huron in the near future. This bit of news brought beaming smiles from both Kristi and Cody whom Maggie had noticed were holding hands whenever they were near each other.

The only event during the two weeks of the exhibit which might have cast a show over the festivities actually turned out rather humorously.

There was a woman from Mitchell named Marlene Manson who owned an art gallery there. She also offered art classes in her studio. Marlene was the self-appointed doyenne of the art circles in both Huron and Mitchell. She appeared at the exhibit almost daily, usually with an entourage of women seeking enlightenment in the world of art. One day Maggie was passing by Marlene and her troupe who were standing in front of a pencil drawing of a coyote. Maggie heard Marlene say, "If I had this boy in class for a few weeks it would much improve his work, this coyote would seem much more alive."

Maggie had heard enough. She barged into the middle of the group and standing with her hands on her hips said, "Marlene you are full of it. Truth be told, you could profit from observing Cody's work a little more closely. If that coyote looked anymore alive it would jump off of that paper and bite you on your big fat butt."

At that, Marlene expelled a sharp, "Well," and marched out of the shop. She was not seen at the exhibit for the remainder of the show. Maggie received a rousing round of applause from the crowd in the store and a warm hug from her mother who happened to be present.

Chapter 40   2169

One day in September Phoebe answered a knock at her door to find three young women who looked vaguely familiar. She could not put names to the faces but was certain she had met them before. All three of them began to speak at the same time then stopped in embarrassment after which they introduced themselves one at a time as Judy, Trish and Joyce.

Now Phoebe remembered them. They had been teenagers in New Home when Brendon and Phoebe had moved to Huron. They had been inseparable as children and often claimed that something from the past bound them to such close friendship. They had felt some of the same attraction to Lori Brown but had discounted it due to the age difference.

The young women told Phoebe they had a story to relate. They had brought the story to her because she and Brendon had been mentioned in the story.

The day before the three of them had set out for Brookings by car. About ten miles east of Huron the car had, with no warning, stopped running. They had called Judy's father and he told them he would be on his way in minutes. While they were waiting Joyce noticed a large glass jar which was half buried in the ditch. There appeared to be papers rolled up in the jar. Using a stick they loosened the sand and gravel from around what turned out to be a gallon jar, then lifted it from the ground. The lid appeared to be stainless steel or aluminum and showed no rust. The lid had been sealed in place with epoxy or some similar material.

That night they laboriously scraped the sealant from the lid and managed to open the jar. Inside they found a single sheet with a handwritten note, two spiral bound notebooks plus a number of personal papers. The notebooks appeared to be journals.

Trish, speaking for the group, told Phoebe they had brought the papers to her because she and Brendon had been mentioned in the journals. The papers were spread out on Phoebe's dining table and it was suggested she read the single page note first.

"To the person reading this, my name is Brian Benson. It is late May of 2108. I don't know the exact date. I have been wandering since April 2106 looking for other survivors. Given what I now know I will be heading for Mount Vernon, Washington. Three days ago I came upon two people beside the road. She was dead and he was dying. He would accept no sustenance except a little water. He told me his name was Calvin and he was ready to join Carolyn. He said their story would be found in two journals and where the journals and personal papers were to be found in their van. Within two hours Calvin had also died. I read part of the journals then wrapped the bodies in blankets and buried them beneath the jar holding this note. If this note is ever found the remains should be reburied in a place of dignity and honor. These two people were true heroes."

Phoebe now turned to the first journal knowing what she would find. As expected, early in the book she found the account of she and Brendon's encounter with the Campbells. She closed the book and asked the young women if they could point out the spot where they had found the jar. They assured her the location was well marked.

Phoebe then told them the material should be shown to Chris so it could be incorporated into his book concerning the survivors. It should then be sent to the National Archives to be preserved for the future.

In due time the remains, now consisting only of bones and a few scraps of cloth, were dug up and cremated. The remains were placed in a single urn and held by Phoebe. George was asked and he created a small granite monument which was placed uphill from those already existing in the pasture. It was engraved with the names of Calvin and Carolyn plus the words, Helpers – Heroes.

Chapter 41 2170

It had been a mild winter and spring came early. By the middle of March the buffalo herd was gone on its annual migration. Chris was soon aware of just how much time he had spent sitting and watching the animals. At eighty-six years of age he didn't walk anywhere he could take his electric cart. It held three people plus a small box in the rear for carrying whatever he needed to transport on any given day.

Cody was till a frequent visitor. He was feeding the prairie dogs at least once a week. He was now giving them a sweet commercial cattle feed instead of Gram's cookies. It was actually less expensive and it certainly saved Phoebe a lot of time in the kitchen. Cody was a busy young man. He spent two days each week at his Aunt Maggie's gallery. His work was in demand and people came from all over the country to see him work at his drawing table. Most people were surprised at his appearance upon meeting him. A few tried to take advantage of his limitations but were met head-on by his fiercely protective Aunt Maggie. Those people were quickly shown the door and were refused the opportunity to purchase a drawing at any price.

One day in April Chris received a phone call asking if a group of five people could stop by to discuss a political matter. The caller stressed that it was important for Linda Ann to be present for the meeting.

Two days later Chris was seated on the deck occupied in his favorite morning activity. He was feeding Chickadees from his hand when a helicopter clattered overhead and landed in the pasture behind the house. Chris did not personally know any of the five people who approached the house. He was, however, aware of who they were. There were two women and three men. One of the women was Dr. Dustin White the Vice-President of the New United States. The other woman way Kaijah Hall the junior Senator from Indiana. The three men were all U.S. Representatives from Kentucky, Mississippi and Alabama. After introductions were made two tables were pushed together, the five visitors seated themselves on one side and opened the cases each of them was carrying. Dr. White then spoke. She asked whether Linda Ann was present and if she could join them. Chris replied that he was sure Linda Ann would be out shortly. As if on cue Linda Ann appeared pushing a cart laden with a coffee urn, cups and a large tray of cookies and sweet rolls fresh from the oven.

After everyone was served Dr. White opened the conversation by saying, "We are here at the request of the President. On the first of May there will be a vacancy on the Supreme Court. Justice Brown is in failing health and has tendered her resignation effective on that date. We have thoroughly looked at the ranks of the judiciary and those who are practicing law. It is our opinion that Linda Ann is the best qualified person in the law community to fill that position. If she will accept the position the President is prepared to present the nomination to Congress. These four people from the Congress assure us that the nomination will be confirmed on the first ballot."

There was a moment of silence then Linda Ann spoke. "This is an honor and position I have wanted my entire adult life. You must realize however that my father is eighty-six years old and needs assistance in his daily life. I will not abandon him for any position." Senator Hall now entered the conversation. She said, "If we have been presumptuous please forgive us. We have discussed this at some length and thought this might be your position. We have been in touch with Chris Jr's daughter Brenda who told us she would love to come and take care of her grandfather. We are aware of the fact that Brenda is a Lesbian but do not see that as a problem unless the family objects." Now Chris spoke, "For the record, both public and private, it should be known that

Brenda is a lovely, intelligent young woman who is loved and cherished by every member of this family."

So it was settled. Linda Ann was headed for Lexington and the U.S. Supreme Court. Brenda was coming to Buffalo Run to look after her grandfather. She also hoped to help further Cody's artistic career. She had been working as a curator at the new Art and Science Museum in Lexington and had been able to acquire a few of Cody's drawings for display there. He was referred to by the museum staff as the Prairie Portraitist.

Chapter 42 2170

Shortly after the disaster of 2106 the Cherokee and Choctaw people in Oklahoma had moved en masse to eastern Tennessee and western North Carolina. This area had been the ancestral home of the Cherokees. They had settled in, built homes and occupied several small towns and cities. They planted large gardens and captured many of the cattle, swine and chickens which were running wild so they ate well.

Perhaps the major drawback to the situation was this was a well-educated group of people. There were many of them with advanced degrees in law, the various arts, engineering, medicine and the sciences. These individuals were not content in being gardeners and small farmers. By the time they were contacted by the Scout Team in 2130 they had already sent out their own scouts to look for suitable areas.

After much exploration and seemingly endless discussion they decision was made to move the population to western South Carolina. The area was virtually void of people and contained not only an abundance of good farm land but many manufacturing facilities as well.

Because of its central location in the area the city of Greenwood was designated as the capital. Work was begun at once to restore Lander U. to the status of a working university. The young people who had been going to Alabama, Mississippi or the Midwest to obtain a higher education now could remain close to home for their studies.

From the beginning the two tribes had lived in mixed communities and merged their business activities. The young people in particular paid little or no attention to tribal lines. They associated with whom they pleased and married as they saw fit. After fifty years the tribal lines were so blurred that the names Cherokee and Choctaw were seldom used. They simply referred to themselves as The People.

By 2165 there were five textile plants operating in the area. Two of them were producing woolen goods, two others were processing cotton and the fifth was manufacturing a new synthetic which had been created in the labs at Lander. The two principal ingredients of the new material were cotton and natural gas. The other ingredients plus the process itself were closely held secrets pending a patent application. The material held all of the attributes of cotton plus it didn't shrink, was longer wearing and could be made in any permanent color desired.

When the subject of statehood was brought up the people along the coast, primarily around Charleston, demurred. They were reluctant to create a state which was certain to be dominated politically by the Native Americans.

Undaunted, The People arbitrarily set eastern boundaries as highways US 20 and US 77 then applied to become the state of West Carolina. In due time the process was completed and West Carolina was admitted to the Union as a State. There was a small population of white people within the new state. A number of these were elected or appointed to various state and federal offices. In what was perhaps a "tongue in cheek" attitude the motto of the new state was to be, The People's State.

Chapter 43 2171

Chris came wide awake and his bedside clock told him it was 3:30 am. This was unusual as he normally slept soundly until around seven. As he lay I bed a feeling of unease came over him. At four he eased out of bed and shuffled towards the kitchen.

As he passed Brenda's always open bedroom door she called out, "Grandpa are you alright?" "So much for being quiet." Chris thought as he replied, "Yes I'm fine, just wide awake, so you can go back to sleep." Chris closed Brenda's door then went on to the kitchen where he turned on the already prepared coffee maker.

When the coffee was ready he filled a cup and a thermal carafe then went outside to await the dawn. The early birds were already beginning to stir and by five o'clock they were at the feeders. The chickadees, as was their habit, flew down to the table where he was sitting to be hand fed. One of them, and Chris thought it was the same one every day, alit on his shoulder then hopped down and explored his shirt pocket for the three or four sunflower seeds Chris had put there.

Brenda brought breakfast for both of them and they ate while listening to bird chatter and the scolding bark of a squirrel down in the aspen grove. As they were finishing Chris became aware of Melinda making her way along the walk between the houses. At the age of ninety-one Melinda was as slim and erect as she had been as a young woman when Chris had first met her in Wyoming some fifty-seven years ago. She now walked with a cane but still moved at a brisk pace.

As Melinda climbed the ramp which had been built to replace the steps Chris and Brenda could see that her eyes were red from weeping and there were tears on her cheeks. Brenda jumped to her feet and placing a hand under Melinda's elbow helped her to a seat next to Chris. Chris immediately asked, "Is it Brad?" Melinda nodded her head yes, then began to speak. "We had a wonderful evening yesterday. We talked about growing up on the reservation, of medical school and most of all about our family and the many friends we have had over the past years. We went to bed happy and content with our lives. This morning Brad simply didn't wake up. I am pleased that his last day was such a pleasant one and that he was at peace with the world. After so many years together I am going to miss him terribly but my children and their children will help fill the void."

They sat quietly for a few moments until Brenda broke the silence. She said, "Aunt Melinda, I want you to come and live with Grandpa and me. We have plenty of room and you shouldn't be alone." Chris immediately added his voice to the request and after pondering the matter for a few moments Melinda said, "Yes, that would be nice I think."

While they were discussing the service to be held for Brad, Cody appeared on the walk. As he came up the ramp it was obvious that he also had been weeping. His eyes were red, his cheeks wet from tears and his nose was running. He hugged and said, "I love you," to all three of the adults. Then, with no preamble he told them his Gram had gone to be with Gramps during the night.

Melinda moved to a double seat then reached for the boy and pulled him down beside her. They held each other and quietly wept for some time. Chris and Brenda looked on and wept with them. Finally Cody pulled a large bandana from his pocket and after mopping his face, passed it to Melinda who did the same. With a rueful smile Cody then said, "No more cookies for Cody and the prairie dogs."

Brenda spoke up. She told Cody she had his Gram's recipe for peanut butter cookies. She added that while her cookies might not be as good as Gram's, she was sure the prairie dogs would find them edible. She told him she had baked a batch just yesterday and suggested he get his scooter and go see if the cookies were acceptable. Cody told her he would rather walk. He had seen a new lizard last week and wanted to find it again to make sure he had the colors correct when he drew it.

Chapter 44 2171

The decision was made to have one service for Brad and Phoebe. There would be a substantial number of people coming from Iowa, Colorado and other points. Most of them would be attending to pay their respects to both of the deceased so it just made sense to combine the services. There was no church in the area capable of seating the anticipated crowd so it was planned to hold the service in an elementary school gymnasium. Even so, there was not enough seating and more than a few people leaned against the walls around the perimeter of the gym. The urns were displayed on a small table and behind each was a colored pencil portrait drawn by Cody.

People were invited to speak and the program lasted for more than two hours. Much was said about the kindly care of Dr. Sweet who had remained in his practice and on twenty-four hour a day call into his ninety first year. Phoebe was praised for her pioneering spirit and her unceasing efforts to create and maintain a good public education system. Cody insisted on speaking but was so overcome with emotion that all he managed to say was, "Goodbye Gram, I love you."

Later that evening Brenda, Melinda, and Chris were having cocoa and peanut butter cookies from Phoebe's recipe. Chris and Melinda had been discussing events from the dark days of 2106. Melinda turned to Brenda and said, "You have no idea what this man means to me. Aside from my husband he is the best friend I have ever had. Your grandmother Carol was a close second but I owe your grandfather for my entire adult life. It has been a wonderful experience and if I lived for another ninety-one years I could never repay or thank him enough." As Brenda was rinsing cups and cookie plates Melinda approached Chris. She clasped him in a fierce hug and kissed him soundly on the lips after which she whispered, "Thank you."

Chapter 45 2171

The next morning at nine Brenda went to check on Melinda who had not yet appeared for breakfast. This was unusual as Melinda was known to be an early riser.

Brenda found Melinda in her bed. It appeared as if she had died peacefully while holding a picture of a younger Brad.

Chris immediately called Pearl and Janis who had spent the night in Brad and Melinda's house next door to Chris. Neither of the women was surprised at the news. They had spoken at length with their mother after the service for Brad and Phoebe yesterday. Melinda had repeatedly stated that she and Brad had shared almost eighty years together and she had no desire to go on without him. Aaron or as he was known to family and friends as A.R. would not be home for the service. He was currently on a boat in the Aleutian Islands looking for a suitable facility for his growing fleet of crab and halibut boats.

The service for Melinda was held two days later. The number of people in attendance was almost equal to that for Brad and Phoebe. Many tributes were paid to Melinda with perhaps the most moving being that given by three members of the Cheyenne people. They spoke of her being the moving force in the building of a modern hospital in Yuma and the training of doctors to staff the facility. They also stressed that the generosity of Chris had provided the majority of the financing for the project.

Chris retired late that night. He had been devastated by the loss of Melinda. She had been his oldest friend and the only other surviving member of his generation of the family and circle of friends. Brenda had sat with him and encouraged him to talk while plying him with herbal tea in an effort to get him to relax.

Chris spoke of the many kindness Melinda had shown others. He also spoke of the steel in her makeup, mentioning the confrontation with the group of outlaws when the clan was moving to Alabama. Eventually Chris became tired he was slurring his speech. Brenda turned down his bed and after he had changed to his pajamas tucked him in and kissed him good night. She told him if he wakened in the night and needed anything to use the newly installed pager to call her.

Chapter 46 2106

Chris came awake slowly. Even before his eyes opened he knew he was not in his bed at home. When he did open his eyes his surroundings were dim and out of focus. As his vision improved he could see that he was in a hospital room. His left arm was loosely strapped down with an I.V. taped in place. His right leg was encased in a cast from ankle to mid-thigh and was suspended by wires from an overhead bar.

Hanging from the railing by his right arm was a small panel with four buttons on it. He could not see what was printed beneath the buttons so he pushed all of them. Within seconds lights were flashing and a bell was ringing out in the corridor. Suddenly there were four people crowding around his bed. A young woman in a nurse's cap took his wrist to check his pulse while another put a stethoscope to his chest and listened intently. Both of the nurses smiled and a young man who turned out to be the resident doctor for the ward said, "So you decided to come back to us, you have had us worried." The doctor then said, "You have a feeding tube down your throat and can't speak. I am going to ask you a few questions which can be answered yes or no. Blink your eyes once for yes and twice for no. Can you do that?" Chris blinked once. The questioning was very short in duration. It quickly became apparent to the young doctor that Chris was not in a mental condition to follow the questions or compose even yes or no answers.

The doctor told Chris that both the orthopedic and neurosurgeon would be in to see him soon, patted him on the shoulder and as he was turning to leave told him if he needed anything he should pus only the large black button on the panel.

The doctor had administered a mild sedative through the IV to help Chris relax from his agitated state. He was half dozing when a slight noise and motion at the door caught his attention. There were two people entering the room and as he focused on their faces he gasped and felt as though his heart was going to jump from his chest. It was his parents but he knew that was just not possible. They were dead. He had buried them sixty-five years ago with his own hands.

His mother, Alta Jean, rushed over to the bed and clasped him in a warm embrace followed by a kiss. His father, Daniel, also hugged him and kissed him on the cheek. Alta pulled a chair over beside the bed and sat where she could hold his free hand. Alta said, "I know you can't speak with that tube in your throat. You will never know how happy we are just to see your eyes open. We have been her almost every day since you arrived. Your eyes were always closed but we could see the eyes moving under the closed lids. Dr. Weaver said that was a good sign as it indicated brain activity. We need to be going as I can hear the doctors in the corridor. We received a phone call from Carol this morning and she will be here tomorrow morning. The medical group finally found a substitute and Carol is on her way home, to stay, she said." With that, Alta gathered her purse plus Daniel and was gone.

Six people entered the room. One was the resident from the earlier visit. His name identified him as Dr. Browning. Two of them were older and Chris assumed the other three were interns making round with their mentors. One of the older men stepped over, took Chris by the hand and said, "I am Dr. Weaver, it is a pleasure to have you back with us. I am your neurosurgeon, this other gentleman is Dr. Gatling, the orthopedic wizard who put your leg back together. The first thing we are going to do today is remove that feeding tube and see how well your voice works. Expect it to be hoarse and raspy but be assured it will be back to normal within a week."

With that the two doctors stepped aside and watched while the interns removed the tape holding the tube in place then gently pulled the tube out and put it aside. Dr. Gatling then told them to remove the IV line as it was no longer needed. When this was completed Dr. Gatling told Chris they had taken pictures the previous day and the leg appeared to be healing well. It was his intention to leave the cast in place for another week just to be sure it was no longer needed.

Dr. Weaver then explained to Chris that he had sustained a severe blow to the back of his head. X-rays indicated there had been no skull fracture but the event had ripped loose a large portion of his scalp and left it draped over his forehead and eyes. They had shaved his head and sutured the scalp back in place. "That has healed nicely but you now resemble a bald man with a zipper on his head."

In a raspy voice he scarcely recognized as his own Chris asked, "What happened?" Dr. Weaver replied with a question of his own. "You don't remember the plane crash?" On hearing the words, "place crash," it was as if a switch had been turned on. Chris stiffened in his bed and closed his eyes. After a few seconds his eyes opened. He then said to the doctors, "I remember every detail of the accident, right now I am tired and my throat hurts. Can we talk about it tomorrow?" Dr. Weaver assured him they could wait for the next day and told him if he needed relief for pain or help in going to sleep that night he should call the nurse and it would be provided.

Later two male aides entered the room and told him it was bath time. They removed the catheter from his bladder and the diaper he had been wearing. After giving him a warm bath and dressing him in clean pajamas they changed all of the bedding and pronounced him ready to meet the world. Chris confided to them that he had been somewhat embarrassed as it had been years since anyone had washed his behind for him. The young men laughed and proceeded to tell him about a bawdy elderly woman who had insisted they be the ones to bathe her. She had giggled and laughed and when they were finished she asked if they provided home service. Sadly she had passed away only a few weeks after leaving the hospital. Both of them were convinced she would have been an awesome grandmother.

By lunch time Chris was ravenously hungry. His face apparently showed his disappointment when he was presented with a large cup of cream of chicken soup and a milk shake. The aide patted his arm and told him his throat was still too tender to accept solid food.

Chris spent the early afternoon hours reviewing and reliving the event of April 7. He had lifted off of the Dallas Center airstrip at 5:45 am and started a climbing left turn to put the plane on a heading of due west. When the compass indicated the correct heading he leveled the plane and continued his climb. He had just glanced at the altimeter which indicated an altitude of 750 feet. Suddenly there was dead silence in the plane except for the noise of the wind whistling past the windows. Both engines had stopped and there was no power to his instrument panel. The landing gear had been retracted and he was too low to attempt turning for a landing at the airport. Losing altitude rapidly Chris managed to just clear the power lines along US 169. He was over what appeared to be a field of oats some six to eight inches tall. There was a heavy dew on the oats and when the plane touched down the dew seemed to add a hydroplaning effect. The plane slid along on top of the oats without digging into the soft ground.

Chris could see that the plane was going to go into the timber before it stopped or slowed much. Without really thinking about it Chris accepted his fate, folded his hands in his lap and waited for the end. As the plane entered the trees it slid between two sturdy maples which sheared off both wings. It then went over something which lifted the nose just enough to clear the trunk of a giant cottonwood which had fallen. The fuselage dropped solidly on the log and broke cleanly apart just behind the cockpit. The nose dropped back to the ground and still remaining upright, continued to skid along the ground. When it finally came to a dense growth of young trees the remains of the plane had slowed enough that Chris could actually see the nose skin begin to crumple as it slammed into the trees. At that point darkness overtook him and he knew no more. Both wings and the fuselage had burst into flames when the plane came apart.

The fire and rescue plus the ambulance crews had been out in front of their building watching when Chris took off. They were still watching when his engines quit and the plane started down.

They were in their vehicles and moving when the fire erupted. The fire and rescue teams arrived at the crash scene in a matter of minutes. They were surprised to find the nose section fairly intact and thirty yards away from the fire. It took them a half hour to cut Chris out of the crumpled wreckage. He was in the ER of the Dallas Center hospital scarcely an hour after the crash. The ER doctor took one look at the x-rays of Chris's leg and stated that this was a case for Dr. Gatling at University Hospital in Iowa City. Within an hour Chris was in a high speed helicopter bound for Iowa City. Dr. Gatling had spent eleven hours putting the leg back together using titanium plates and screws. Another team had shaved his head and sutured his scalp back in place. Through all of this Chris had remained unconscious but his vital signs remained steady and normal.

Chapter 47 2106

When the hospital shift changed in late afternoon Dr. Browning escorted his replacement for the night shift into the room to introduce her to Chris. On seeing the new doctor Chris was speechless and almost went into shock. She was a slender young woman with brown skin and vivid blue eyes. Her name tag identified her as Dr. M. Swift. She took his wrist and looked at her watch as she checked his pulse. She placed his arm back on the bed, looked at his chart and commented that his heart rate was a little high. Chris blurted, "That is because of you, you could be the twin of someone I once knew for many years. Is your name Melinda?"

The doctor smiled and told him that was a new line she had not heard before. She then told him her name was Melanie but her husband and friends called her Mel.

That evening when the clatter of supper was over Dr. Swift returned to the room and pulled a chair over to the side of Chris's bed. She took his pulse again after which she commented that she must be losing her touch since his heart rate was back to normal. She then said, "Tell me about this Melinda who could be my twin. Chris told her about meeting Melinda and some of the events in the life they had shared as friends.

Dr. Swift listened to him careful then said, "Today is May 10, 2106. You have been with us for thirty-three days and I think you have been dreaming for most of that time. I think you should see Dr. Bevin's. He is the head psychiatrist here at the hospital and he is famous for his study and work with dreams."

Melanie now changed the subject of their conversation. She told Chris she hoped they could become good friends as she suspected they were going to become neighbors or at least near neighbors. She and her husband Bart both felt there was too little medical service for the rural areas of central Iowa. When she finished her residency in two months they planned to open a clinic in the north part of Dallas County. Bart had already finished his training and was currently helping out in a surgical ward at a hospital in Cedar Rapids. The plan was contingent on finding the financing for constructing the facility. Chris replied that she may have already found her financial source. His grandfather John, who lived in Adel, was probably the wealthiest man in Dallas County. Chris had heard from John many times bemoaning the fact that rural people had to travel too far to obtain quality medical help. A word or two from the right person might resolve the financial question and Chris thought he knew whom that person might be.

In the middle of the night Chris was dozing, only half asleep, when he was jolted wide awake. He was sure he was listening to the opening chorus of Wolf Song from his dreams. After a few seconds he recognized the noise as a squeaky wheel on a custodial cart passing his door. This was soon followed by a husky whisper from Melanie telling someone to get a can of oil and lubricate that wheel before it awakened all of her patients.

Chris awoke at six-thirty in the morning to the sound of voices outside his door. He recognized one of the male aides who had bathed him the day before. The young man said, "Ma'am there are absolutely no visitors allowed on this floor before seven-fifteen. This is the I.C.U. and these patients need all of the rest they can get." The female voice which replied was one which Chris had not heard in two years but which he recognized instantly. It was Carol, who replied to the you man by saying, "I compliment you for your devotion to duty but you need to know that as of now I am Mr. Weddle's primary care physician. If you do not step aside and allow me to enter that room I am going to start shouting loudly enough to awaken every person on this floor."

Chris turned on his bedside light and called Carol's name. She rushed into the room and sat on the side of the bed. She covered his face with kisses and more than a few tears. After a bit she put her head on his chest and wept quietly. Chris soon realized that Carol was asleep. He lay quietly with his arm across her shoulder and was both relieved by and thankful for her presence. In her sleep Carol moved about until only her feet were extending over the edge of the bed.

Dr. Browning was making his first round of checking on patients. He had been told that Chris had an early visitor but nothing more than that. When Dr. Browning, whose first name was Steve, saw the woman in the bed with his patient he immediately assumed it was the doctor whom Chris's mother had spoken of yesterday. The two men began speaking very softly but it was enough to awaken Carol. She sat up and after looking at Steve's name tag apologized for being in bed with his patient. She explained that she had only wanted a hug but after sixty hours of travel with no sleep she simply gave in to the need to close her eyes and rest. Steve told her there was a room available for the family of patients to rest but she refused the offer. She told him Gramps had a three bedroom suite reserved at a nearby hotel. She was going there to sleep for a few hours and would return in late afternoon.

For breakfast Chris was served scrambled eggs, toast with apple jelly and a cup of mixed fruit. He couldn't remember when anything had tasted so good.

Drs. Weaver and Gatling entered the room at the same time. Dr. Gatling went directly to the point of the visit. He told Chris he had reviewed the pictures of the leg again and was convinced it was healed enough to remove the cast. Chris would then be moved to a new room and would start on a vigorous regimen of exercise to strengthen the leg. He warned Chris there would be some pain as the muscles and tendons would have to be stretched to avoid a limp.

As Dr. Gatling was removing the cast Dr. Weaver presented Chris with a cycling helmet. He told Chris the only way he would agree to discharging him from the hospital in less than two months would be for Chris to agree to wearing the helmet at all times, except when he went to bed at night. Chris readily agreed and donned the helmet. When the cast was finally off he was slid onto a gurney and wheeled along several corridors to his new room.

It was a bright, sunny room with a large window through which one could see the Iowa River just to the east. Chris was immediately placed sitting on the side of the bed and his rehab was started at once. He was asked to do some simple movements to test the flexibility of his ankle, knee and hip. The joints were pronounced as satisfactory and he was told the serious work would start tomorrow.

As Chris was being served his supper that evening Carol came into the room. With the aide standing nearby Carol planted a demure kiss on his cheek then took a seat and waited quietly. When he had finished eating and the dishes taken away Carol said, "Chicken noodle soup for a man recovering from an accident is ridiculous. Tomorrow you are going to have fried chicken, mashed potatoes with gravy and probably dessert from your mother's kitchen." With that said she locked her fingers in his bike helmet and kissed him long and thoroughly.

Carol stepped back then said, "Now that you know how I feel I have two questions. Do you still want to marry me and if so, how soon?" Chris, somewhat dazed by the passion in the kiss replied, "Yes and as soon as possible." To that Carol said, "Good, your parents and Gramps will be here at eleven in the morning. They will be accompanied by the proper people with correct documents. We can apply for, receive the license and be married before noon." She then said, "Your mother and grandfather seem to be able to pull strings that other people don't recognize as being strings. I will see you around ten in the morning. Goodnight." With that she was out of the door and gone.

Just after seven that evening a man whom Chris did not recognize walked into the room. He was short, gray haired and had eye glasses perched on top of his head. The man introduced himself as Dr. Bevins and said he had been asked to speak with Chris about his dreams. He stressed to Chris that he didn't attempt to interpret dreams but sometimes he was able to help the dreamer discover what had brought them about. They talked for two hours with the Doctor encouraging Chris to recall his dreams with as much detail as he could remember. When Dr. Bevins finally left Chris was totally exhausted. He soon turned out the light and was almost instantly asleep. The nursing staff noted that he spent a restful night, apparently undisturbed by dreams.

Chapter 48 2106

Chris was awakened at 6:30 the next morning. He was immediately given his breakfast along with the comment that he
had a busy day ahead.

At 7:30 the two aides who had tended him in the ICU entered
the room. They explained that they were Physical Therapists
who had been temporarily assigned to the ICU. They reminded
him their names were Tom and Jerry and their last name was
Dunhill. Their purpose was to help him learn to walk again.

They spent an hour doing simple knee bend exercises with
both legs. There was some pain with the right leg but actually less than Chris had expected. After the hour Tom and Jerry
bathed and shaved him, changed his bedding then announced
that he was as ready for his bride as they could make him.

Promptly at 10:00 Alta Jean and Carol swept into the room
with three men in tow. Two of them were clerks from the county
office while the third was a minister from the hospital chapel.
Papers were signed, notarized and fees paid. Tom and Jerry were
called in to sign and act as witnesses. In less than an hour a somewhat dazed Chris was a married man.

After they were finally left along Carol sat on the side of the
bed, took Chris's hand and said, "We need to talk. As you know,
I am twenty-four years old. I want to have my babies, four of
them, by the time I am thirty. I will not try to have my way with
you while you are here recuperating but when we get to go home
to our own bed be prepared to do your duty. We need to get
Chris Jr. started soon. Also, unless you have major objections I
would like to take a partnership in the clinic Melanie and Bart
plan to open. I would like to ask your mother to plant a hint with

Gramps about financial backing. You know he is unable to say no to her about anything."

Chris smiled, then replied, "I don't have much experience and certainly no recent practice but I will do my best to help you with the baby thing. As for my grandfather, he has even less resistance to you than he does with my mother. He just growls at you to see those gorgeous green eyes flash wide open. In either case I would guess your financing is secure."

That evening, true to her word, Carol carried in a basket containing a feast. It contained fried chicken, mashed potatoes, green bean casserole and glazed carrots. All of it fresh from the kitchen Alta Jean had set up in the hotel suite with hot plates and a toaster oven. She had been afraid they would be ousted for cooking in the suite but a few words between Grandpa John and the hotel manager had cleared the way.

Chapter 49 2106

The rehab for the leg seemed slow to Chris but after two weeks he was walking with a cane and only a slight limp. By the first of June he could walk for a half hour on the treadmill with no sign of a limp and without overtiring himself.

On the tenth Dr. Gatlin told Chris he could go home. The doctor cautioned Chris about over exerting the leg and told him to walk for two half hour sessions every day. Dr. Weaver had his say as well. He wanted Chris to wear the cycling helmet for another month. He told Chris that after such a serious head injury another severe blow could send him to a place from which he might never return.

Dr. Bevins saw Chris almost every day. He could not account for Chris's dream which spanned sixty-five years. Drs. Weaver and Blevins both agreed there must have been some little spark in the brain which refused to die. By keeping itself alive it had, by extension, kept the body alive as well. Dr. Blevins told Chris he had a rehab assignment for him to work on. He told Chris that after he had been home for a few weeks and had settled into his new role as a husband he wanted Chris to set aside some time every day and write an account of his dreams. The doctor wanted him to write every word he could recall and every event both major and minor. Dr. Bevins didn't know if his account would explain anything about a dream spanning sixty-five years. He was sure that it was unusual enough that it should be recorded and studied.

Chapter 50 2106

I t was a typical Iowa late July day. The thermometer was standing at a steady 96 degrees and the humidity nearly matched it. Chris was seated under an umbrella on the deck with a glass of iced tea at his elbow. He could hear Carol singing in the kitchen as she prepared an apple pie from his mother's recipe.

He had been considering where to place his writing desk. It was time to start the writing task assigned to him by Dr. Bevins. He knew putting it in the house was not an option. Carol could not walk past him without patting his arm or kissing him on the ear. He loved every touch from her but knew he would be distracted for at least a half hour after each one. He knew that would not be conducive to a productive writing session so he would have to do his writing out of her sight and reach. He had about decided he would use what had been designed as a tack room in the little three stall horse barn. It was well lighted plus it was air conditioned. Chris was about to go out to the barn to check the tack room. He wanted to see what needed to be done to make sure it was usable as a writing space. He had just risen to his feet when an old but well-kept truck pulled in and stopped in front of the machine shop. The first thought to enter his head was that the truck had to be twenty years older than himself. As the driver got out Chris recognized him as Charlie Wilson who lived a mile and a half east. Chris waved and called out, "Mr. Wilson come up here where we can sit in the shade.

The elderly man made his way to the deck, shook Chris's hand and took a seat. Without any preamble he began to speak. "I apologize for not stopping in sooner. I am sort of a loner and most of the time I would rather be by myself. I heard about your accident and I'm sure you can use some help around the place. Your ditches are badly overgrown and in bad need of mowing plus you have twenty acres of Timothy and Alfalfa hay which should be cut and baled. I have the machinery and would be more than happy to do those two tasks for you. You will need to hire some help to get the hay into the barn." The old man paused then continued. "That is the longest speech I have made in years but I need to start being a better neighbor." Chris thanked Charlie then told him if he wanted to cut and bale the hay it would be his as Chris had no livestock.

Carol wheeled a serving cart out to the deck. It was laden with pitchers of iced tea, lemonade and a carafe of coffee. The three of them sat and chatted for the better part of an hour. They were interrupted only when Carol went inside to take her pies out of the oven. When Charlie, he insisted the call him Charlie rather than Mr. Wilson, was preparing to leave Carol presented him with a pie in a cloth carrier. She told him he would have to come back for another visit when he returned the carrier and pie plate.

Charlie's truck had no more than driven out of sight around the corner of the driveway when two others appeared. In the lead was Alta's little electric car followed by a big new pickup driven by Grandpa John.

Carol bounced down the steps then hugged and kissed Chris's parents. She then turned to John and give him a fierce hug followed by a firm kiss while saying, "Thank you Gramps." Chris greeted his parents then turned to John and said, "It is good to see you again so soon Gramps." John snorted then growled, "I have asked you not to call me Gramps. It makes me sound like an old geezer. I may be getting old but I am not a geezer yet." Chris was somewhat surprised by the rebuke. He turned to his grandfather and said, "But mom and Carol call you that all of the time and you never say anything." John answered him by saying, "Your mother does it just to show me that I don't intimidate her. With Carol, if I growl as her it brings on that puppy which has just been kicked look and I just can't do that to her." Alta chimed in with, "John you are just an old softy and deep down you know you love it that Carol and I call you Gramps."

As they settled around the table and everyone had a fresh glass of tea or lemonade, Alta spoke. "I can read in their eyes that both Gramps and Carol have news for us. In deference to his age I think we should let John be first. The floor is yours Gramps."

John stood and began speaking. "The Medical Center is underway as we speak. We have purchased two hundred acres, one hundred sixty of which will be dedicated to the campus of the medical center. The remainder will become parks or housing. That is yet to be determined. The property begins at the road a mile west of Dawson. It is bordered on the south by highway 141 and stretches to the north to the timber above the river. The initial phase will consist of three two story buildings of twenty thousand square feet each. The three doctors who were primary physicians for Chris in Iowa City are all near retirement age. They have been retained as advisors for matters concerning building layout, equipment and staffing. To help our three young doctors get their feet on the ground and a patient base established we are going to erect three pre-fab buildings in Dawson to be used as temporary offices. The surveying crews started work today and the architects have been busy for the past week. That is all I have to tell you today. Carol, I believe it is now your turn."

Carol now stood and said, "I have only three words that matter, we are pregnant. My home test was positive yesterday and today. I will see a doctor next week to confirm the fact but I am already certain."

After a supper of chicken, baked potato and sweet corn, all cooked on the grill by Chris, they finished with the apple pie Carol had prepared. Alta Jean told Carol she had the recipe tweaked to perfection and not to change anything. After the elders departed Carol and Chris sat out on the deck and watched a full moon rising in the east. They had been in bed sleeping for some time when Chris bolted upright in the bed. He wondered for a moment if he was back in one of his dreams but saw Carol sleeping beside him and knew that he was at home in his own bed. Then he heard the sound which had awakened him. It was the unmistakable ululating cry of a wolf. He sat listening and knew it was not possible. There had been no wolves in Iowa for almost a century. Chris left the bed as quietly as possible and went out to the deck where he stopped to listen more. There was no mistake, it could be nothing but two or three of the big predators howling almost at his back door.

He heard Carol open the door then she joined him on the deck. She slipped her arm through his and leaned against his hip. They listened together for a bit then Carol whispered, "Now you can truly name this place Wolf Song as you did in your dreams."

They went back to bed but sleep proved elusive for Chris and he dozed only fitfully for the rest of the night.

Chapter 51 2106

Chris arose when the first hint of dawn began to lighten the room. He felt groggy and slightly disoriented from lack of sleep but knew his night was over. In the kitchen he started the coffee then returned to the bedroom and dressed for the day.

Chris had decided he was going to put his smokehouse to use. The previous fall he had cut down and trimmed twenty each of hickory and hard maple trees then dragged them into piles beside the smokehouse. He had also acquired some apple wood from an orchard where new trees were being put in.

Carrying a thermal cup of coffee Chris walked out to check the log piles and make plans for how to attack the task. The first problem he faced was how to get the logs onto the sawbuck so he could start cutting the thirty inch pieces required by the firebox.

As Chris was contemplating this problem he heard then saw a truck in the driveway. It stopped in front of the machine shop where Chris had left the door open. Chris began to walk in that direction but stopped short when the driver stepped out of the vehicle. The man seemed vaguely familiar and Chris immediately thought of his distant cousin Brendon from his dreams. The appearance was similar even to the unruly shock of red hair on his head.

Chris stepped up, thrust out his hand and said, "Good morning, my name is Chris Weddle, I don't believe we have met before." The newcomer grasped the proffered hand with a firm grip and replied, "My name in Brandon Hintz and my wife and I will be your new neighbors as soon as we get moved. We bought the Bates place a half mile west last winter. The out buildings were in good shape but the house was a total wreck. I have spent the spring and early summer rebuilding the house and now we are ready to move in. I know about your accident and now that we will be next door neighbors I would like to offer you my help in any way I can." Chris suggested they walk up to the house for fresh coffee and for Brandon to meet Carol. Brandon agreed but said he could not stay long as the movers were due to arrive at 9:30 and he didn't want Phyllis to think he had abandoned her.

Carol was elated at the prospect of having neighbors. She had been feeling somewhat isolated and having another woman nearby would be comforting. She insisted that rather than spending the day moving then having to prepare a meal Phyllis and Brandon come to her house for supper. She said she would invite Chris's parents and grandfather plus Charlie Wilson so they could all become acquainted. Chris could grill chicken while she and Alta prepared the rest. They would not eat until 7:30 to give the Hintzs a chance to unwind from what would be a hectic day. Everyone accepted so Carol had the task of entertaining a group in her new home for the first time.

The evening went well. Alta brought a variety of fresh vegetables from her garden and the chicken was done to perfection

After they had finished the meal and were chatting over mundane things Brandon dropped a bombshell into the conversation. He told them he had the genealogy charts of his family and if you went back five generations he and Chris were cousins. Their ancestors of that generation were a twin brother and sister. John considered this for a while then spoke, he said, "I remember my father Dallon mentioning that he had cousins named Hintz. There were three brothers named Aaron, Ryan and Brad. Their children, at least the ones I recall, were named Hunter, Hudson and Persephone but I don't remember which child belonged to which brother. I do remember that Hudson had the middle name Elliott. I never met any of them and I presume their families are still in Washington." Now Alta entered the conversation by asking Brandon what had brought him all of the way from Washington to Iowa.

Brandon told them he had finished high school at age sixteen then enrolled at WSU which he attended for three years and graduated early with a degree in Ag. Engineering. All of the time he was in school what he really wanted was to be farming. On returning home he had rejoined the family farming business which by then had become a full-fledged corporation. He soon became disillusioned with corporate agriculture. He wanted to make the decisions on which crops to plant in each field and when to market them. He looked around and finally decided to start over in Iowa.

Brandon had been able to purchase the Bates place which was only twenty acres in size and without a livable house. He had spent the winter trying to rent farm ground but it seemed no one was willing to trust their land to a man only twenty-three years of age. He was capable with tools and was able to make an adequate living doing carpentry, plumbing and simple electrical jobs.

On hearing this statement Chris told Brandon that if he had time the next morning to come back. Chris had a remodeling job which needed to be done immediately.

Conversation had tapered off and for the most part the group sat listening to the night sounds in the woods around the house. The Cicadas were in full voice and the night birds were twittering. From far off in the timber a Great Horned Owl hooted from time to time. When the sound Chirrs had been hoping to hear began, everyone sat on the edge of their chairs and listened intently. The wolf chorus continued for a full half hour. During that time no one spoke a word. When it was over the silence continued until John spoke. He said, "Wolves. That was the first time I have heard them since my last hunting trip to Alaska in 2085. I had no idea there were any of them in Iowa."

Carol spoke next. "That settles it. We are going to name this place Wolf Song as Chris called it in his dream."

Chapter 52 2106

The next morning Chris and Brandon examined the tack room. Brandon pointed out that if he moved two walls it would give Chris much more room for his writing studio. In three weeks Brandon had created a twelve by sixteen foot room with a counter to hold a coffee machine and space for a small refrigerator. The outside wall was opened and a small window was replaced with a large one to provide a view of the woods to the north. When the building, actually a horse barn, had been erected Grandpa John had insisted a toilet be included so that problem was already solved. A computer and telephone were installed, both wireless, and with carpet on the floor the studio was ready for use.

Chris wavered over the process of the actual writing. He could type on the computer but it was a two fingered process and very slow. In the end he decided to write with a pencil on yellow legal pads then look for a skilled typist to put the text into the computer.

In October the three young doctors moved into their new offices. The buildings had been put up on a corner of Main Street in Dawson. Bart had been on the computer researching the history of Dawson. He discovered that the corner where their offices sat had been the location of the last doctor to practice medicine in Dawson over one hundred-fifty years in the past. Consequently they had a sign made and erected which read, Doc Elliott Medical Clinic.

The three young doctors were well aware of their limitations due to inexperience. They recruited three middle aged and well respected physicians to join their practice and act as advisors.

When the U.S. Surgeon General heard of the facility under construction west of Dawson she moved quickly. With support from Congress she proceeded to pay John for his investment to that point. Experts were put to work planning with the result being a three hundred bed hospital and major research facility.

Chapter 53 2106

On the last Friday in October the group, at John's request, got together for a cookout dinner at the home of Chris and Carol. Alta Jean and Phyllis provided most of the food. The meat was ribs provided by Lance Handly, a forty year old engineer who was expected to oversee the opening of two new composite plants in South Dakota and Alabama. The locations were still undetermined but Huron or Mitchell were favored in South Dakota and Montgomery in Alabama.

John had sampled the ribs at a company potluck and wanted to share the delicacy with his family. The ribs were a resounding success and there were immediate requests for the recipe for the sauce. Lance was reticent in answering but his wife Elizabeth spoke up. She said, "We don't want to appear selfish but Lance spent fifteen years perfecting that recipe and we consider it a family secret. We will provide bottles of the sauce to anyone who asks for it but the recipe will remain a secret."

John stood and took the floor. He spoke primarily to Chris and Carol. He asked them if he could have perhaps two acres of property on which to build a small house. He added that if he was going to have great-grandchildren he wanted to be close enough to spoil them without having to drive all of the way from Adel.

Chris replied that of course he could have however much property he wanted. If he would spend the night with them they could go out first thing in the morning and select the site.

John now directed his remarks to Brandon. "Brandon I have been observing you closely for five months, both here personally and by correspondence in South Dakota. You are intelligent, hardworking and from all appearances honest. In addition you are family. I have a proposition for you. Two miles south of here is a section and a half of land which will be for sale next month after the last of the corn is harvested. Eighty acres are in pasture with a creek rambling through. The remaining acreage is all till-able except perhaps five acres containing a good set of buildings minus a house. My proposal is this. I will buy the property and you will farm it. After expenses we will share any profits half and half. After five years if I deem you have fulfilled your part of the agreement I will deed the entire property to you and your wife. Tomorrow after Chris and I look at the property here for my new house you and I will drive out and look at the farm to see if it meets your expectations."

There was stunned silence on the deck until Brandon finally found his voice. In almost a whisper Brandon said, "Mr. Weddle I don't know what to say except a heartfelt thank you. I don't even need to see the property, my answer is yes right now."

John spoke again, "Nevertheless we will go look at the farm tomorrow. One other thing, I don't like being addressed as Mr. Weddle by family. You are too young to call me John so why not be like Chris and call me Grandpa."

Phyllis was on her feet in an instant. With a sly smile she asked, "Does that mean I can call you Gramps as Alta and Carol do?" Melanie was next, she stood and addressed John, "What about me? I know I am not family but I haven't had a grandpa since I was eleven."

John threw his hands in the air and said, "Oh what the heck. The women in this group sure know how to take advantage of an old man's good nature. Just don't tell everyone how easy I am, Gramps it is." Every one of the young women including Alta walked over and gave the old man a warm hug and resounding kiss.

They sat talking quietly for a while. It had turned quite chilly and they had all bundled up in coats with some of them in caps as well. Chris had been talking about a picnic shelter he wanted to build on the lip of the hill overlooking the river. He wanted lots of glass on both the north and south sides with sliding doors to let in the air when the weather permitted. Alta commented that she would like to see this supper held once a month. Especially after the little ones began arriving. It would assure her of seeing them at least once a month and she was ready to begin her role of being a grandmother. Charlie Wilson added his wish to see the babies come along also. Charlie, who had always seemed quite reticent with his speech now turned voluble. With no coaxing he told them he had married at a young age. He and his wife had two babies in rapid succession. Both of them had been still-born and shortly after the second one his wife had committed suicide with an overdose of sleeping pills. He had withdrawn from the world and with the exception of his younger brother Jack seldom spoke to another human.

It was obvious that Charlie was not finished speaking but at this point the Wolf chorus began. Everyone sat quietly and listened. They didn't hear this every night but it was a regular event two or three nights every week. When it was ended, Adrianne who was the nine year old daughter of Lance and Elizabeth spoke up. "That was beautiful. It was as if they were singing for us. I am going to put this in my diary as the night of the Wolf Song Supper. I hope we can have more of them."

John had accepted Carol's invitation to spend the night. He always carried a bag in his truck containing a change of clothing, underwear, pajamas and a toiletry case. Dan and Alta had lingered after the other guests had departed. The five of them were having a late cup of de-caffeinated coffee. Alta, who was known to speak her mind, told the others she felt it was time for Charlie Wilson to have some female friends in his life. He was only fifty-six and she felt no one should grow old with no family and no friends. She was a member of the Dallas Center garden club and there were several single ladies in the club who were of an age to be "friends" with Charlie. She would work something out.

The next morning John was up at dawn. He was anxious to be about his tasks for the day. Carol insisted that he wait and have breakfast before going out to look for a home site. It took less than an hour for them to find the spot for which John was searching. Less than three hundred yards from Chris and Carol's house a finger of land stretched north between two wooded gullies. They paced the width and John declared it broad enough for both a house and garage.

John insisted they get Carol's opinion before settling on this spot. They walked over to get Carol to come and look. It was Saturday so she was home rather than at the clinic. After walking over the site she told John it was a perfect location. He could even put up a covered bench out at the tip from which to watch the river. John told her he didn't want her to feel as if her privacy was being invaded. Carol patted his arm and told him it couldn't be better. If she ever needed an emergency baby sitter all she had to do was step out on the deck and shout, she wouldn't need a phone.

Chris called Brandon and told him Grandpa was ready to look over the farm. Brandon was there within minutes. Chris declined the invitation to accompany John and Brandon. He told them the arrangement was between the two of them and he would remain mum until they had settled the details.

During the drive out to the farm John spoke, he said, "I spent a lot of time thinking last night and I have changed my mind about what we discussed yesterday." Brandon tried not to react but a disappointed sounding, "Oh" escaped his lips. John continued as if he had not heard the "oh" from Brandon.

"You are family. My father Dallon, who founded our company, always admonished me to share the wealth we were accumulating. My plan is this. I will buy the land and deed it to you free and clear immediately. This winter we will find someone to advise you and purchase the equipment you will need to farm this much acreage. For the first two years I will furnish seed and fertilizer plus pay the operating expenses including your living expenses. If you will plant the varieties of corn and soy beans we require to manufacture the composite material we will pay you ten percent above market value when you decide to sell."

John drove into a parking area in front of a neat, well maintained set of buildings. Before Brandon got out of the truck he turned to John and said, "I accept your offer. How could I not?" They made a cursory inspection of the buildings including the spot where the house had once stood. It had burned some twenty years before and was never replaced.

On arriving home Brandon immediately, with Phyllis in the truck with him, drove back out to what would be their farm. They examined the buildings closely and walked the fields. Brandon pointed out the old house site and told her they could build a new one if she wanted to live on the place. Phyllis told him she would rather stay where they were and commute the two miles to the farm. She liked her neighbors and suspected there would soon be more. She confided that Melanie and Bart had told her they were going to ask Chris to sell them enough space to build a home in the edge of the woods. Even if Chris didn't want to sell more property he would not be able to resist once Melanie flashed her smile and sparkling blue eyes at him.

Carol asked and Brandon agreed to make a sign for the entrance to the community. Carol made a sketch and Brandon told her he would execute it in Western Cedar.

Chapter 54 2107

In January the doctors from Iowa City who had been seeing Chris every month since the accident told him they wanted him to give up his pilot's license for a least five years. Following a severe head injury there was always a change of a seizure or blackout with no warning symptoms. Dr. Bevin's who was continuously urging Chris to start writing the story of his dreams finally insisted on a starting date for the project. They finally settled on February fourteenth.

John, who was flying to Montgomery or Huron almost weekly needed a regular pilot to replace Chris. He hired a newly retired USAF veteran with more than twenty years' experience at the controls. Is name was Phil Black and he soon asked for permission to build a home in the woods just east of where John's house would be.

Both the existing well and solar array belonging to Chris were adequate to supply water and electricity to all four houses. What had been a single house set alone in the edge of the woods would now be in the center of a five house community which spanned a half mile. Carol was ecstatic over the prospect of having neighbors.

One day as Chris got out of his car in front of the clinic he was approached by a man who had driven in just behind him. The man introduced himself as Jack Wilson. He told Chris he was looking for the home of his brother Charlie and all he had for directions was an RFD route number which wasn't much help. Chris gave him detailed directions and asked him to have Charlie call Chris on his cell phone later in the afternoon.

When Charlie called Chris asked him whether if he had an hour or so to spare in the next day or two. Chris would like his opinion on a project he and Brandon were working on. Charlie asked if he might bring his brother and sister-in-law. They were visiting and he didn't wish to leave them sitting alone. They agreed to meet in two days. When Charlie had mentioned that Jack's wife was named Martha, Chris had an instant flashback to his dreams. He was still four days from his promised start date to begin writing but he vowed to himself to start the next morning.

What Chris wanted from Charlie was his opinion on the pork hanging in the smokehouse. He and Brandon had agreed to share two hogs Brandon had furnished and which Chris was smoking.

Alta had stopped in to check on Carol who was in the eighth month of her pregnancy. When Charlie and his guests come to see Chris, Alta invited them to come with Charlie to the community supper the following week. Charlie had looked at the meat and suggested two more weeks of smoking should be just about right.

Chapter 55 2107

When Chris finally sat down as his desk to begin writing he found he was at a total loss. Where to begin? He wanted the story to unfold in chronological order but soon realized that was probably not going to be possible. He decided that he would write whatever came to mind on any given day and put it all in order later.

Consequently, the narrative of his dream odyssey began in October of 2113 which was seven years after it actually began. The writing continued for the better part of six months. At times Chris wrote at an almost frenetic pace while sometimes a week would pass without a single word being put on paper. Meanwhile life went on.

Chapter 56 2107

On the day of the community supper Brandon came up the driveway towing a long trailer. Chris, accompanied by now waddling Carol, went out to greet him.

Brandon told them he had something to show them and wanted to know on which side of the driveway they wanted it placed.

In the trailer was a three by twelve foot sign. Three cedar planks had been fastened into a frame and then carved in deep relief. In the center was a depiction of a full moon and at each end was a howling wolf with nose pointed at the sky. On a smaller board fastened to the bottom of the sign were the words "Wolf Song." Chris stared in speechless amazement while Carol, who had known what was in the trailer, smiled and patted his arm. Chris clasped Brandon in a brotherly hug and related thank you several times. Brandon replied that it was only a small thanks for what Grandpa John and by extension the Weddle family had done for himself and Phyllis.

As people began to arrive in late afternoon they were all complimentary over the newly installed signs. Since all three of the young women were in the advanced stage of pregnancy they were told to sit and visit. Alta, with the assistance of Elizabeth and Martha, had prepared the meal with the exception of the meat. Lance had been prevailed upon to grill pork ribs and chicken breasts.

On this night there was no wolf chorus. This omission was discussed and John expressed the opinion that the noise from the heavy equipment working on roads and preparing home sites had probably spooked the animals. Charlie agreed and felt that when the building was complete the wolves would probably return.

Adrianne announced that she was still going to call this the Wolf Song Supper and hoped there would be more of them. Lance spoke up and announced that he and Elizabeth were looking at a place just to the west of Brandon and Phyllis. It had a good sized house which would need to be remodeled on the inside. The property included five acres of pasture plus a two stall horse barn. Adrianne had been campaigning for a year for a horse or pony and this seemed like perhaps a good time and place for that to happen. Adrianne chimed in again with, "Besides I could baby sit for all three of my aunts."

Alta who had been waiting for an opening, addressed Charlie. "Charlie I saw your yard and flower beds last spring and I don't believe I have ever seen a prettier place. You must have every flower and shrub which does well in Iowa. Where did you learn all of that?" Charlie, somewhat embarrassed, replied, "By watching my mother tend her yard. She was a master at selecting and tending plants. I do it now in her memory." When asked when the blooms were at their peak he replied, "Usually around May tenth."

Alta explained that she was a member of the Dallas Center Garden Club and she would very much like to bring the club to see his yard in full bloom. Charlie told her to pick a date and give him a few days' notice so he could have everything neat and trim for the ladies. He then asked if the ladies would expect tea and cookies as had been the habit of his mother's group. Alta told him she would take care of the refreshments but Charlie told her not to bother as he needed to make cookies once in a while to stay in practice.

Chapter 57 2107

Alta had already moved a crib, cradle and boxes of baby clothing from her attic to Chris and Carol's home. It seemed she had saved everything. The crib had been purchased at the time Chris was born. The cradle was an heirloom built by an ancestor some one hundred-twenty years in the past.

Beginning with Carol on April 25 then Melanie and Phyllis on May 3 and 4 three babies were added to the community.

Carol named her baby Chris Jr. Melanie gave birth to a girl and named her Kaijah. Phyllis also gave birth to a girl and named her Mavis.

Alta, Martha and Elizabeth spent most of their waking hours tending to the mothers and babies.

On the appointed day a ten passenger bus driven by Phil Black pulled into Charlie's driveway. Alta was already feeling pleased with her plan. She had noticed frequent contact between Phil and her friend Karla Browning. She was sure Phil had winked at Karla at least once and Karla had responded with a warm smile. They were greeted by A Charlie whom Alta almost did not recognize. She had never seen him dressed in anything except overalls and rough work shoes. Today he was wearing slacks, polished loafers and a bright red polo shirt.

The tour of the yard began immediately. There were many questions from the women about the flowers and shrubs. They were familiar with all of the plants except one. It was a low growing shrub with spindly woody stems. The flowers were medium sized with a single row of pink petals. There was much speculation as to what it might be. Charlie finally told them it was a rose, an Iowa wild rose dug out from the edge of the timber along the river. When asked which brand and types of fertilizer he used on the various plants Charlie told them he never used a commercial fertilizer. The sole additive to the black Iowa soil was horse manure gathered from his pasture and horse barn. When they had finished the tour of the yard and flower beds Charlie invited them to walk down by the barn to see his pets.

Alta told Charlie that while he was at the barn with the others she would go in the house and start preparing for tea if he didn't object to having a strange woman in his kitchen. She asked him where she would find cups. Charlie told her in the cabinet just to the left of the coffee machine. Alta entered the house to find a dining table with eight chairs plus a small table with four seats. Both tables were covered with lacy linen cloths. She went to the cabinet really expecting to find an assortment of chipped and stained coffee mugs. What she found was a tea set with at least eighteen exquisite cups and saucers. There were three matching tea pots, a box of spoons and three each silver creamers and sugar bowls. In the panty she found several trays of dainty sugar cookies plus more robust looking molasses ones. Alta had printed place name cards at home. She now put these in front of each chair. She seated the two men at the small table with her friends Karla and Kristi. It was all she could do without being obvious about her goal and she didn't want to embarrass anyone.

As the group outside neared the pen beside the barn Charlie loosed a piercing whistle then said, "They will be here in a minute or so." In a matter of moments a pair of sorrel Belgian horses came trotting up the lane from the pasture. The people lined up along the fence and the horses stopped, facing them. Charlie said, "The one with the black streaks in her mane is Belle, the other one is Beau." Kristi extended her hand and Belle stepped forward, sniffed it, then extended her head across the fence and rested in on Kristi's shoulder. Charlie said to Kristi "That means she likes you plus she wants a sugar cube." Slipping a sugar cube into the hands of both Kristi and Karla, Charlie told them to hold them in their palms and show them to the horses. Both horses picked up a cube with just their lips and commenced crunching them. Before moving away Belle brushed her velvety muzzle against Kristi's cheek. Kristi remarked that she believed the horse had kissed her. Charlie was tempted to say it might be a pleasant activity but held his tongue and let the moment pass.

The tables were set with cookies, cream, sugar and a variety of tea bags. Before Alta poured the first ceremonial cup she spoke to the group. "We have always been a ladies only group. I am not proposing we change that. What I would like to suggest is that we make Charlie an honorary member. He has a wealth of information from which all of us could benefit. Also we wouldn't need to feel guilty about taking up his time." Kristi was on her feet in an instant saying, "I would like to second that proposal. I was going to ask him anyway but this would make it easier."

A vote was taken and the proposal was passed unanimously. A shout of speech, speech was raised so Charlie reluctantly got to his feet and spoke. "I accept and thank you ladies for you confidence in my talents. I do have a question however. Does the designation of "Honorary" mean anything other than I can't vote on issues?" As Charlie took his seat Alta noticed that Kristi reached out and patted his hand then left her own hand resting on top of his. After sitting for a few moments Charlie rose to his feet again. First he apologized to the ladies for breaking into their conversations then told them he had just remembered something which had been an important part of his mother's club meetings. He stepped into the pantry and emerged holding two fancy decanters plus a bottle, the label of which identified it as an imported French brandy. He placed the decanters on the large table and the bottle on the small one. "Mother always said a sip of good brandy helped to seal whatever decision had been made. Help yourself, or not, as you please and thank you for coming." When Charlie sat down again Kristi reached out and took his hand. She also moved just enough that their knees were touching. The observant Alta took note of this, "Like a lamb to the slaughter," she thought, "a lamb to the slaughter."

Chapter 58 2107

The babies were doing well. Both Carol and Melanie had taken six weeks off from their practices to recover and to insure the little ones were off to a good start. Both babies were nursing and the mothers planned to continue that. A room at the clinic was set up as a nursery and a nurse was hired to take care of the little ones during working hours.

Chris went to his writing desk every day. The dreams were still vivid in his mind and flowed from pencil to paper with almost no conscious effort. His only problem was in attempting to relate the dreams to his real life. For instance he was greatly perplexed by the people. It was beyond his reasoning ability to correlate the names of the people in his dreams with those who had entered his life since awakening. There were so many of the real people with names which were identical to those of his dreams.

Dr. Bevins was a frequent visitor. He avidly read the accounts written by Chris but could offer no real insight as to the root cause of the dream. All Chris really knew was that he had gone to bed one night as an eighty-seven year old man nearing the end of his life and had awakened as a twenty-two year old with most of his life still ahead of him.

Dr. Bevins told Chris that when it was published this story was going to be the fodder for many studies for years to come.

Chris now had twenty-three legal pads filled with his dream memories. After reading it twice he decided against doing any re-writing but divided it into three volumes.

He decided to title the works "The Journeys Trilogy." Volume I was titled: "The Journey to New Home", Volume II was to be: "Wolf Song The Journeys Continue", Volume III was: "The Awakening New Journeys."

The End

Elliott Combs is a pseudonym for Harold Elliott Weddle. I grew up using Elliott as my name because of a preference by my mother. Her maiden name was Combs. When a friend insisted I must have a pen name, my maternal grandfather came to mind. His name was William Daniel Combs so the author became Elliott Combs. The military insisted on first names, so everyone I have met since 1952 knows me as Harold.

I grew up in the little Iowa town of Dawson. After a hitch in the Air Force, I enrolled and graduated from Clemson University in South Carolina. I spent most of the next 31 years teaching various Industrial Art Classes plus Math and U.S. History.

When I started writing in 2012 I decided to make Dawson, Mount Vernon, Washington and Huron, South Dakota prominent locales in the books.

Many of the names used are those of family and friends, but not necessarily in the context of when I knew them in the past.

Writing the books of the "Journeys Trilogy" has been great fun. I hope the reader gets as much enjoyment from reading them as I did in putting them on paper.

Elliott Combs, October 2015

Made in the USA
Charleston, SC
25 May 2016